TOM SWIFT AND
HIS SPACE SOLARTRON

The silvery missile was streaking toward the dome!

The silvery missile was streaking toward the dome!

THE NEW TOM SWIFT JR. ADVENTURES

TOM SWIFT
AND HIS SPACE
SOLARTRON

BY VICTOR APPLETON II

ILLUSTRATED BY GRAHAM KAYE

GROSSET & DUNLAP PUBLISHERS

NEW YORK

PRINTED IN THE UNITED STATES OF AMERICA

CONTENTS

CONTENTS

CHAPTER I

MORE POWER!

"CALLING Tom Swift!"

"Power failure in the wind tunnel!"

"Hey, the presses have stopped in the metal-stamping department."

Excited voices blared out over the loud-speaker in Tom Swift's private laboratory at Swift Enterprises' vast experimental station. The telephone was jangling shrilly. A lanky, blond youth of eighteen with deep-set blue eyes switched off his experimental equipment and scooped up the receiver.

"Tom Jr. speaking."

"For Pete's sake, take it easy, skipper!" gasped a voice at the other end of the line. "You've popped the main circuit breaker!"

"The load's off," Tom reported. "I just stopped my experiment."

As he hung up, a husky dark-haired youth burst into the laboratory. "Hey, what's going on,

1

genius boy?" Bud Barclay demanded. "Are you trying to sabotage this place?"

Tom grinned wryly. "Relax, Bud. I was just running a test on my new matter-making machine. I arranged with the power plant to cut in the stand-by generator, but even that wasn't enough to handle the current load."

Bud slumped down on a lab stool and mopped his forehead. "Whew! I thought someone was blowing up the joint! Even the radio tower started to—"

Suddenly his voice trailed off and he stared at the young inventor. "Did you say a *matter*-making machine?"

Tom chuckled at the surprised look on his friend's face. Bud Barclay was his closest chum and acted as copilot on Tom's air and space flights.

"That's right, pal," Tom explained. "This pilot model rigged up on my test bench is designed to turn electrical energy into matter."

Bud shook his head. "Man, that'll be a better trick than pulling a rabbit out of a hat. You'll be making something out of nothing!"

"Not exactly." Tom grinned. "You wouldn't call an atomic explosion *nothing*, would you?"

"I'd say it's nothing to fool around with," Bud quipped. "Why?"

"Well, with atomic fission, you're turning matter into energy. This setup does just the reverse. Both cases depend on Einstein's famous equation $E = mc^2$, which means that energy and matter are interchangeable. They're simply two different forms of the same thing."

Bud scratched his head thoughtfully. "Like water and ice, I suppose. Sounds good, but how do you do it?"

Tom grabbed a pencil and paper. "It's quite simple, really—at least the idea is simple. Einstein has shown that as matter approaches the speed of light, its mass increases. He worked it all out in this one little equation."

As Tom's pencil flew over the paper, Bud gulped. "You call that one *little* equation, pal? Looks like a whole night's homework in math to me! Keep it simple, please."

"Okay." Tom laughed. "What my new invention does is take a particle of matter and whirl it around faster and faster until it's going almost at the speed of light."

"And the faster it goes, the greater its mass?" Bud asked.

"Right. In my experimental rig, the results only show up as a slight increase of mass on this platinum screen that I'm using as a target. But I'm building a new model which I hope will produce enough matter so that I can actually weigh it."

"Wonderful, professor!" Bud exclaimed, slapping his pal on the back. "But what's this machine for—a scientific magic show?"

"No," Tom replied. "It's to help us explore space—perhaps colonize the moon."

Bud's eyes grew round with excitement. "Now

you're talking my language, skipper! Give me the low-down!"

"Well, on the moon, or when we're traveling through space," Tom explained, "we'll be cut off from our source of supplies. If this machine could produce oxygen, water, maybe even fuel and food, then we could exist away from the earth as long as we wanted to stay."

"Wow!" Bud bounced off his lab stool. "That means we could *really* explore space, Tom—even visit the farthest planets!"

The young inventor nodded, grinning. "Exactly. But don't get your hopes up too soon, pal. My machine isn't perfected yet, and I'll need a lot more power to carry out my experiments."

Tom was interrupted by a third voice. "Wal, brand my buckshot, next time try an' carry 'em without blowin' all the *ee*-lec-tricity on this here spread!"

The boys looked up with broad smiles as a chunky, bowlegged, weather-beaten figure came into the laboratory. Chow Winkler, the Enterprises cook, wearing a white chef's hat and high-heeled cowboy boots, was pushing a lunch cart in front of his ample midriff.

"Sounds as though you've had some trouble, Chow," Tom said sympathetically.

"Trouble? Pardner, I've had real misery! And all on account o' your experimentin'. My mixer went dead jest when I was beatin' up some lemon meringy. My electronic range wouldn't work. An' there I was with two dozen half-baked pie shells."

Chow grunted with disgust as he served the food off the cart. "So there's your lunch, wranglers—cold beans an' applesauce."

"Looks good to me," said Tom, as both boys piled into the food hungrily.

"It better be, son, 'cause that's all I got to offer. Jest lucky you didn't electrocute yourself into the bargain, messin' around with all them volts an' killywatts!"

Tom chuckled silently. He knew that under the old Westerner's leathery hide beat a heart as warm as Texas sunshine. Chow Winkler had been a chuck-wagon cook when he met the Swifts during one of their atomic research projects in the Southwest. He had become so fond of Tom that he agreed to go back to Shopton with them and take on the job of chef for the Swifts at Enterprises. When they went on expeditions, he usually accompanied them as cook.

"In case you didn't know it, Chow," Bud put in slyly, "Tom's inventing a new way to make all your groceries, so you won't have to take any along on our next space trip."

Chow glared at the young copilot. "None o' your whoppers, Buddy boy!"

"It's true," Bud insisted. "He's going to make all our food out of electricity."

"Out o' *ee*-lec-tricity!" Chow's tanned, lined face went pale with dismay. "Great jumpin' Jehoshaphat, boss—is that true?"

"Well—in a way," Tom replied hesitantly.

"Brand my buffalo stew!" Chow groaned. "You

think I can fry up *ee*-lec-tricity on a cookstove, or sling up a dish o' boiled electric current? Why, first thing you know, I'd be blowin' the space-ship—"

"Whoa! Hold on, Chow!" Tom interrupted with a grin. "It's true that I'm trying to produce matter from electrical energy, but that doesn't mean you'll have to cook up any volts or amperes." He explained his invention briefly as Chow listened with a worried frown. "And besides," Tom ended, "I don't even know yet whether my invention will pan out."

"Wal, let's jest hope we don't all wind up gettin' *carried* out—on stretchers!" Chow grumbled darkly.

Still chuckling, Tom finished his food, then picked up the phone and called the Shopton Power and Light Company. He asked the manager if arrangements could be made to increase the supply of power to Enterprises from the town's generating plant.

"Sorry, Tom," the manager replied. "Our facilities are already overloaded. I'm afraid we can't help you until we get our new reactor plant built."

"I understand. Well, thanks, anyhow," the young inventor said and hung up.

At that moment Tom's father came into the laboratory and both boys jumped to their feet as they said "Hello."

There was a close resemblance between father and son, especially in their keen, blue eyes, but

Tom Jr. was the taller and rangier of the two. After Mr. Swift had seated himself on a stool, the boys sat down and Tom told his father about the power failure.

"No luck with the electric company?" Bud asked.

Tom shook his head. "Looks as though I'll have to go out to the Citadel if I want to continue my experiments." The Citadel was the Swifts' great atomic research center in the Southwest. "With our new generating plant out there, I should have all the power I need."

"That might be your best bet, son," Mr. Swift said. "By the way, why not take Ted Spring along?"

"Good idea, Dad. If he's going to accompany us on future space flights, he may as well familiarize himself with this project. I'll phone him."

A few minutes later Ted Spring reported to the laboratory. Twenty-two years old, he was tall and athletic with light-blond hair. After graduating from an aeronautical engineering school, he had taken special training as a space pilot before joining Swift Enterprises.

"Hello, Mr. Swift. Hi, fellows!" he greeted them. "What's up? Do I get my first space cruise soon?"

"I'd say you're about ready for it." Mr. Swift smiled warmly. "But first we'd like you to go out to the Citadel with Tom to work on a new project."

There was a warm feeling of closeness between

Mr. Swift and the young engineer-pilot. Ted's father had been not only an old friend but a crack test pilot for the Swift Construction Company. He had lost his life on a recent test flight, and since then Mr. Swift had taken a fatherly interest in young Ted.

"I'm trying to develop a machine which will convert energy into matter," Tom explained. "My test rig here looks promising, but I'll need a tremendous amount of energy to perfect the real model. That's why it's necessary to continue my experiments at the Citadel."

Quickly Tom explained the principle of his new invention and showed the blueprints for his first working model. Ted was greatly impressed.

Mr. Swift put an arm around Tom's shoulder. "Son, this is the most advanced experiment ever undertaken by anyone since the development of atomic energy. I'd say you're on the right track, and if your project is successful, it'll be a milestone in science!"

Tom flushed with pride. "I wouldn't have got this far without your help, Dad," he said quietly.

"Nonsense, son." Mr. Swift smiled. "This is your own project. But let's talk more about it this evening. Ted, will you join us at dinner? You too, Bud."

"With pleasure, sir!" Ted agreed, as Bud nodded eagerly. Both were familiar with Mrs. Swift's hospitality and delicious cooking, and Bud had an extra reason for looking forward to the evening. Tom's blond, vivacious younger sister, Sandra, who was Bud's favorite date, would be there.

As expected, the dinner of fried chicken and oven-hot mince pie was delicious. As Bud and Sandy, next to each other at the table, joked and chatted, Mrs. Swift turned to Ted. A petite, attractive woman, she avoided the public attention focused on her famous husband and son and devoted her time to homemaking and entertaining the many visitors who came.

"How's your mother, Ted?" Mrs. Swift asked solicitously.

"Fine, thank you," Ted replied. Suddenly a worried look shadowed his face. "That reminds me. I had an odd experience the other day."

"What was it?" Tom asked.

Ted said he was embarrassed to mention it but thought the Swifts should know about it. "A man named Hampshire phoned me. He said he was a lawyer and claimed he could get a lot more money for Mother and me, in connection with my father's accident, even though Swift Enterprises had made a large financial settlement.

"You understand," Ted went on, "that we are well satisfied with everything. You folks have treated my mother very generously. But I felt I'd better tell you what Mr. Hampshire said."

"You're absolutely right, Ted. I'm glad you mentioned it," Mr. Swift replied. "What else did this fellow Hampshire say?"

Ted frowned. "That's the funny part of it. He said he wanted no fee for handling the case, just some information in return. Of course I wasn't interested, so I put him off. But since then I've been worried that he might be up to something underhanded."

"I think we should check on him," Tom said firmly.

"I agree, son." Mr. Swift nodded gravely. "Why not call Ames at the plant security office and see if he can trace this Mr. Hampshire?"

"Right, Dad."

Tom made the call after dinner. Harlan Ames, the chief of Enterprises' security department, promised to follow up the matter at once.

"I'll have an answer for you by the time you get back from the Citadel."

The next morning, a sleek cargo jet was rolled out of its hangar and readied for take-off on one of the Enterprises airstrips. Tom checked off the various pieces of equipment as they were placed aboard. Included among these were all the parts for the first working model of his matter maker.

Bud, standing nearby, whistled. "Wowie! Those electric transformers are real giants!" The copilot pointed to several huge transformers, encased in cast-iron "pots," being loaded onto the jet.

Tom smiled. "Yes. They'll be essential for my experiments at the Citadel."

At last, with cargo and crewmen aboard, Tom took his place at the controls. Bud occupied the copilot's seat, while Ted Spring also joined them in the flight compartment. At a signal from the tower, Tom opened the throttle and the jet roared down the runway.

Soon they were streaking westward above the clouds.

Bud grinned with sheer enjoyment. "Space flight or air flight—it's sure a thrill!"

The next instant, all three were startled by a loud crash in the cargo compartment. Then came a piercing scream!

CHAPTER II

SIZZLING METAL

"GOOD night! What was that?" Ted gasped.

"We'd better find out," Tom said. "Take over
the controls, Bud!"

"Roger!"

As the husky copilot focused his attention on
the dials and flight instruments, Tom dashed out
of the compartment. Ted was close behind him.
They made their way along the passage leading
to the cargo hold. Groans and cries of pain continued.

"Something terrible has happened!" Ted muttered.

Reaching the cargo compartment, they saw
that one of the giant transformers had broken
loose from its cradle, pinning a crewman named
Jess Brown against the bulkhead. The flight engineer and radioman were struggling to free him.

"Give us a hand, skipper!" the radioman cried
desperately.

Jess was clenching his teeth to stifle the pain. His face was white, with beads of sweat standing out on his forehead. Tom, Ted, and the other two men strained with all their might to budge the transformer.

"No use," Tom gasped. Flicking on the intercom, he called Bud and explained the situation. "Bank the ship to starboard—but gently or one of the rest of us may get pinned!"

"Roger!" Bud's voice replied.

A moment later Tom and his companions braced themselves as the plane tilted in a wide sweeping turn. Slowly the transformer slid across the deck, back toward its cradle.

"Lash it down pronto!" Tom ordered as he caught the injured crewman in his arms. Hastily the others secured the ponderous cast-iron monster with chains and steel cable. Then, after Tom signaled Bud to right the plane, they helped carry Jess to the nearest bunk. Immediately aromatic spirits of ammonia were held to the crewman's nostrils.

"How is he, skipper?" the flight engineer asked anxiously.

"No ribs broken, thank goodness," Tom announced after a first-aid examination, "but these bruises are bad enough." He got a paper cup of water and some tablets from the first-aid locker. "Here, take one of these, Jess. It'll help to relieve the pain."

"Thanks, skipper," Jess replied. "I'm feeling better already. That whiff of ammonia cleared my head—but it sure hurt like blazes when I was pinned there!"

"You're lucky it was no worse," Ted put in. "You would've been hit full force by the transformer if its flange hadn't caught on a deck girder."

Tom gave the injured man a comforting pat. "Take it easy for the rest of the flight, Jess. We'll have a doctor look at you as soon as we reach the Citadel."

By noon, they were passing over the rugged badlands and desert country which had been chosen as the site for the great atomic research center. Canyons and mesas slashed in rainbow colors by the forces of erosion marked the approaches to the Citadel. Then the terrain flattened out into barren scrubland which stretched away for miles toward the horizon.

"What a layout!" Ted gasped, as Tom lost altitude. "It's as big as Enterprises!"

A vast surface had been smoothed for the atomic plant. A cluster of ultramodern laboratory buildings and dormitories were arranged in pinwheel formation around a massive central structure of white concrete block. The whole installation was ringed with barbed wire and approached by a single desert road. Except for a few Indian pueblos in the distance, no other human habitations were visible.

"That white building in the center is the reactor," Tom explained. "This afternoon, Ted, I'll arrange to have someone show you around."

Six drone planes were circling above the plant. Tom radioed for clearance and brought the ship down on the runway, where an ambulance was waiting to rush the injured crewman to the infirmary. A short time later X rays confirmed that he had suffered no broken bones or other serious injuries.

"Jess is just plain lucky," said Bud as he drove from the medical building in a jeep with Tom and Ted. "What now, skipper?"

"Lunch," Tom decided. "Then to work."

By the time the boys had finished eating, the heavy transformers and other equipment had been unloaded from the plane and trucked to Tom's one-story laboratory building. A crew of company linemen were stringing wire from the powerhouse as the young inventor and his friends pulled up in their jeep.

"Where do you want the pots hung, skipper?" the foreman called down, jerking his thumb toward the transformers.

"Mount them on the roof," Tom called back. "I'll take over from there."

"You'll have a regular substation here," Ted commented. "What's the setup?"

"These high-tension lines will bring in 10,000 volts from the powerhouse," Tom explained, "and the transformers will step that down to 480. You see, my work will require low voltage, but very high amperage."

While the linemen were busy erecting the transformers, Tom went into the laboratory and began setting up the first model of his matter-making machine. Bud and Ted watched, fascinated, as the young inventor worked dexterously.

"Let me see," Tom muttered. "Electromagnet—okay. Castings—check. He turned and glanced at his blueprints. "Vacuum system—than the electronic controls."

"How does he do it?" Ted muttered to Bud. They gaped in awe as the machine gradually took shape.

A dome about two feet in diameter was supported on a column above a broad circular housing. From this, pipes led to the vacuum pump. The controls were enclosed in a separate console studded with knobs, dials, and oscilloscopes.

"Boy, I'd sure hate to have to trouble-shoot this little gadget!" Bud wagged his head.

"Sort of a miniature atom smasher, isn't it?" Ted asked.

"Works on the same principle," Tom explained, "but a better name would be a particle accelerator. An atom smasher uses high-speed particles to bombard a target and cause artificial radioactivity. This machine speeds up the particles just to make them increase in mass."

"And this housing at the bottom is the particle racecourse?" put in Bud.

"Might call it that." Tom chuckled. "The racecourse is actually an electromagnetic field provided by the magnet. We also have to create a vacuum, so that the speeded-up particles don't go bumping into any air molecules."

"Track clear and fast!" Bud quipped. "Which is more than you can say for my brain right now."

"Take a rest, fly boy—you've been overdoing it," Tom said with mock sympathy. "Why not take Ted on a sight-seeing tour of the Citadel while I finish setting this up?"

"Sure. Explaining an atomic reactor should be simple after this." Bud grinned. "Come on, Ted, let's leave our genius to his jigsaw puzzle."

The space cadet laughed. "Okay. See you later, Tom."

Within an hour after his two companions had left, Tom had his new invention completely assembled. Then he drove over to the metalworking shop and forged a set of thick copper bars to carry the current from the transformer to his machine. These, however, proved to be so heavy that he discarded them and constructed new ones of aluminum.

"Nice work, skipper," said Chuck Thornton, one of the shopworkers, as he examined the results admiringly.

Tom nodded. "These aluminum ones are a lot lighter than copper and will handle the current just as well."

Returning to his laboratory, he installed the bars and soon was ready to make the first test run of his matter maker. "Here goes," he told himself tensely.

Switching on the power, Tom adjusted several control knobs. Then he watched the dials with bated breath as the concrete building throbbed with the hum of the tremendous current flow.

So intent was Tom on his experiment that he failed to notice that the aluminum bars were becoming red-hot. As the bars melted under the intense heat, there was a sudden shower of sizzling metal!

"Good night! The circuit's overloaded!" Tom cried out as he fell back, shielding his eyes. Fortunately he was wearing a lab coat of protective fabric. But to turn off the main switch, he would have to stretch his arms straight through the barrage of sparks and molten metal!

"I—I can't reach it!" Tom gasped as he groped vainly for the switch. The white-hot spume of metal was already eating through the fabric of his sleeves, and the exposed portions of his skin stung with agonizing pain!

To make matters worse, he had set up the machine in a corner of the laboratory, and there was no means of escape except through the sizzling metal.

"Help!" Tom yelled.

"Skipper!" a horrified voice cried out. Tom recognized it as Ted Spring's, even though he was too blinded by the sparks to see him. "How can I get you out?" Ted asked frantically.

Tom's heart gave a leap. "There's a big slab of carbon to the right of the door," he called, trying not to yield to panic. "Maybe you can use it as a shield!"

"Roger!"

The slab was several feet long and nearly four

*Sizzling sparks of molten aluminum were
shooting in every direction*

feet wide. Grabbing it up on his palms and balancing it over his head, Ted stooped low and dashed toward the young inventor. The intense heat was like a miniature inferno, with molten aluminum sparks shooting in every direction. Ted managed to insert the carbon slab between Tom and the conductors. In a moment the young inventor had squirmed out of his deadly predicament.

"Give me the slab," Tom ordered, waving Ted back to a position of safety. Approaching the test setup from the opposite side, Tom managed to switch off the power.

He leaned against a bench. "Thanks for saving me, Ted," he gasped, wiping the perspiration from his forehead.

"Tom, I'm taking you to the hospital right away!" Ted announced.

He said nothing about his friend's scorched hair and blistered skin. But he was worried that Tom would be badly scarred and hospitalized for weeks or months.

CHAPTER III

THE MYSTERIOUS CALLER

"DON'T look so grim! I've been burned worse than this playing with other inventions."

Ted forced a smile as he helped Tom outside and into a jeep. "Then it's high time you stopped trying to blow yourself up," Ted retorted. "Don't you get enough excitement rocketing through space?"

Realizing that Tom must be in severe pain in spite of his joking manner, Ted drove to the Citadel's infirmary at top speed. Here a doctor and two nurses took Tom immediately into the examination room.

Bud Barclay came rushing into the infirmary, pale with fright, as Ted nervously awaited the doctor's report. "Just got the word about Tom's accident," Bud panted. "What happened? How is he?"

"I'm waiting to find out," Ted replied. "It could be bad." He gave Bud a brief report of the accident.

Both boys were intensely relieved when the doctor appeared half an hour later and smiled. "You can relax, fellows," he said. "I'm glad to say Tom's burns aren't serious."

"He won't be scarred?" Bud asked anxiously.

The doctor shook his head. "No, the burns are mostly surface—painful enough—but they should heal quickly. Tom will have to stay in the hospital overnight, but I believe we can take the dressings off tomorrow."

"Thank goodness!" Bud sighed.

"May we see him?" Ted asked.

"Certainly, but don't keep him talking too long. Tom's system has suffered a slight shock, so rest is the best treatment now."

As the two boys entered the room, Tom grinned at them through his bandages. He was propped up comfortably in bed.

"What are you trying to do, pal—masquerade as an Egyptian mummy?" Bud asked, grinning.

"The name is King Tut, please," Tom replied. "Down on your knees and knock your head three times against the floor before you address me."

"Sounds pretty lively for a mummy," Ted remarked to his companion.

Bud nodded, pretending to scrutinize the patient with a frowning air. "He'll live, I guess. Once they start wisecracking, it's usually a hopeful sign . . . *Oof!*"

The last remark came in a stifled grunt as Bud ducked to avoid a well-aimed pillow!

"Just wanted to show you my reflexes are still

working." Tom chuckled. "Now sit down and entertain me with your witty conversation."

The three friends were talking and laughing about other things and for the moment Tom's harrowing experience was completely forgotten.

"Good thing no reporter is taking this down for the *Enterprises Journal*," Bud remarked. "He'd think we came out here for a lowbrow gag session instead of a scientific project."

"What's the *Enterprises Journal?*" Ted inquired.

"A new magazine our company's putting out," Tom explained. "It'll be mainly a technical journal, with papers contributed by our research staff and engineers, but there'll be other features too."

"And a real eye-catching cover," Bud boasted. "Sandy designed it. Only trouble is"—he pretended to shake his head in disgust—"I'm afraid the inside may spoil all the good-looking art work."

"How come?" asked Ted with a puzzled look.

"Oh, the technical stuff isn't so bad, but there's one article that'll really make the readers turn blue. It's chockful of Greek-letter formulas and Einstein equations by some long-haired fogy named Tom Swift Jr."

The next moment Bud ducked as Tom let fly another pillow. "Just for that I'll make *you* write it!" Tom vowed.

At this point a nurse looked into the room and stared sternly at the three youths. "Visiting time is up," she announced. "The patient must get proper rest."

"Right." Bud nodded gravely. "I'm sorry to say, Nurse, the patient seems to be getting feverish. Better slip him a double dose of your worst-tasting medicine!"

Tom was still chuckling as his two friends took their leave. Bud's joshing remarks had lifted his spirits and made him feel better already.

That evening as Ted Spring and Bud prepared for bed they heard a knock on the door and a staff clerk entered the room. "There's a long-distance call for Mr. Spring. You can take it downstairs in the office."

To Ted's surprise, the call was from his mother back in Shopton. But his pleasure dimmed when he heard how worried she sounded.

"Ted, that Mr. Hampshire called again," Mrs. Spring reported. "Goodness, I just don't know what to make of it, but I thought you'd better know."

"You're right, Mother. What did he say?"

"Well, he asked for you. I knew that you were suspicious of him, and that Tom Swift and his father would like to trace him. So I said I'd be glad to pass along any message and tried to keep him talking. In the meantime, I told Ray to run next door and call the police on our neighbor's phone, so they could trace the call."

Ray was Ted's ten-year-old brother.

"What happened?" Ted asked, gripping the

phone excitedly. "Were the police able to trace the call?"

"Yes," Mrs. Spring replied. "It was coming from a phone booth in the lobby of some little run-down hotel. But unfortunately the caller was gone by the time a cruise car arrived. This Mr. Hampshire—or whoever he is—had slipped away."

Ted groaned with disappointment. "What a break! Did they get a description of him?"

"Yes, that's one good thing. A bellhop had noticed the man making a call. Said he was a pinched-looking, hollow-eyed man, about forty years old and dark-haired."

"Hmm." Ted mulled over this news. "Well, that's something to go on, anyhow. Are the police looking for him?"

"Indeed they are!" said Ted's mother thankfully. "They're co-operating with Mr. Ames at Swift Enterprises. But so far they've had no luck. There's nobody named Hampshire in the Shopton phone book or any official records. And they haven't found a trace of any visitor in town of that description either."

Ted did his best to reassure his mother about the mysterious Mr. Hampshire. Nevertheless, the young engineer's brow was creased in a worried frown as he replaced the telephone.

He was just leaving the dormitory office when the telephone rang again. Since the clerk had left, Ted answered.

"There's another long-distance call for Mr. Ted Spring," the switchboard operator announced.

"This is Ted Spring speaking."

The operator asked him to wait a moment, then a man's voice cut in, speaking in a high-pitched, nasal whine. "Mr. Spring?"

"Speaking. Who is this?"

"This is Mr. Hampshire," the voice replied. "No doubt you remember that I called you once before. I—"

"Just a minute," Ted broke in suspiciously. "How did you find out where to reach me?"

"That's of no importance. I'm calling to renew my offer of help in the case of your father's accidental death. It so happens that I have some new evidence on that crash."

"Such as?" Ted asked.

"Evidence which has never been brought out before—and evidence, I might add, which would be very embarrassing to the Swifts. Believe me, they would certainly settle out of court for plenty of cash!"

Ted digested this surprising statement. "And what's your interest in all this?" he inquired.

"I'm coming to that," Hampshire went on smoothly. "Now, as proof of my good faith, I'm willing to pass on this information in exchange for some information on your part."

"What do you mean by that?" Ted asked sharply.

"I mean that if you'll just tell me when the *Enterprises Journal* is going to press, I'll give you some inside dope about that plane crash. That's a fair offer, isn't it?"

Ted was startled. What "inside dope" had Hampshire dug up? Ted was curious to learn more, but he mistrusted the caller's motives.

"I don't think I'd care to make a bargain like that," Ted retorted.

"Don't be a fool, Spring!" Hampshire's voice turned nasty. "You're missing out on a good deal. If you think I'm lying, then ask the Swifts about the servo unit on the plane's elevators when it crashed!"

Before Ted could say another word, there was a click at the other end of the line, indicating that Hampshire had hung up.

Puzzled and with an increased feeling of worry, Ted put down the phone and went upstairs to his room.

"Call from home?" Bud Barclay asked.

Ted nodded, and told Bud about both calls, including the sinister remark Hampshire had made just before hanging up.

When Ted had finished, Bud's face flushed with rage. He sprang out of his chair. "The servo unit on the elevators!" he exclaimed. "Hampshire is a low-down troublemaker!"

CHAPTER IV

DANGER ZONE

"TED, that man Hampshire's just trying to stir up trouble to gain something for himself," Bud declared stormily. "All the facts of your father's accident were brought out in the CAA investigation."

"Of course I know that," Ted assured him. He sat down on his bunk and started to take off his shoes. "Listen, Bud, there's no need for you to get so mad. The Swifts treated Mother and me more than generously, and we have no complaints. Our only feeling about the crash was our sorrow at losing Dad."

Bud paced about the room, still red-faced and angry. "But don't you see, Ted—Hampshire is up to something crooked and he's trying to mix you up in it!"

"Well, he's wasting his time." Ted stood up in his bare feet, yawned, and started to change into his pajamas. "If Hampshire *is* trying to pull me into some crooked deal, I'm having no part of it.

The police will pick him up sooner or later. Now let's get some shut-eye."

Bud calmed down considerably, and soon both boys fell asleep. Next morning, however, the husky young copilot was still disturbed by the mysterious phone call. After a hasty breakfast of bacon and eggs in the mess hall, he hurried over to the infirmary to report the situation to Tom.

"Hampshire's a phony all right," Tom agreed, after hearing the story. He chewed thoughtfully on an apple from his breakfast tray. "But I still don't see what his game is. Why did he want to know when the *Journal* is going to press?"

Bud shrugged and hitched his chair closer. "Look, Tom. What worries me is that crack he made about the elevators. You remember the investigation showed that none of the servo units had been tampered with."

Tom nodded. "Sure. And I also remember the findings of the official report. Ted's father got into a slip stream so strong that the servo unit on one of the elevators couldn't stand the high speed. Its booster-control action went out. Without it, Mr. Spring didn't have the strength to control the wheel, rudders, etc. The report concluded that the plane failed under stress, not that any part had been faulty or tampered with."

"Just the same," Bud grumbled, "that guy Hampshire's out to make trouble, and if he tries hard enough, he'll succeed in throwing suspicion on Enterprises."

Tom continued eating his apple for a few moments. "Bud, let's suppose some enemy did tamper with one of the servo units and caused the crash on purpose."

"Okay, let's suppose," his chum retorted.

"If Hampshire does know something, it could be that the *same* person who slipped him the information, may have been responsible for the tampering. In fact, that same enemy may even have planned the whole thing to pry out information on our latest plans and inventions."

"You mean," said Bud, "that Hampshire may be the front man for someone a lot more dangerous?"

"Right!" Tom tossed his apple core away and stared, frowning, out the window at the desert landscape. "It's something to think about, Bud. We'd better be on our guard."

The conversation was interrupted by a "Hi, skipper! How are you feeling?"

The two boys turned to see Ted Spring enter the room. Both Tom and Bud wondered if the telephone call from Hampshire the previous evening might have stirred up any feelings in him of suspicion or resentment against the Swifts. But Ted wore a cheerful smile.

"How's the patient this morning?" Ted inquired.

"Tops!" Tom grinned back. "I can hardly wait till they peel off these bandages."

"Going back to work right away?" Ted asked.

"The sooner the better," Tom declared.

"Swell! I'm eager to see how new tests on your matter-making machine pan out."

"Ditto!" Bud put in. "Boy, if you get that gadget perfected, Tom, we can really take off for the wild blue yonder—Mars next stop!"

"Slow down, spaceman." Tom chuckled. "It'll take a while yet before we're ready to go planet-hopping. If you fellows really want to help, though, there's one thing you can do."

"Name it," Bud said.

Tom reached out to the night stand beside his bed and picked up several papers covered with pencil sketches. "I've designed a cooling apparatus to keep those aluminum conductor bars from overheating," he said. "You two might rig it up this morning."

Tom explained the drawings, and his friends eagerly promised to tackle the job.

"Consider it done, skipper." Bud clicked his heels and snapped a quick salute.

Between them, Bud and Ted assembled and installed the apparatus in a couple of hours. When they returned to the infirmary after lunch, the boys found Tom dressed and his bandages removed.

"Hey! The patient's fully recovered!" Bud chortled, grabbing his pal in a bear hug.

"Ouch! Take it easy!" Tom's face assumed a comical expression of agony. "The nurse says I'm to be treated extra delicately."

"Okay. I'll put on kid gloves for our next

match," Bud bantered. "Just incidentally, the cooling apparatus is all set up for your test run."

"Swell!" Tom's eyes lighted up. "Let's go, pals. I want to give that machine a real workout! Why, for Pete's sake! Chow!"

"Whoa! Slow down, buckaroos!" Chow's fog-horn voice boomed from the doorway. He stumped into the room on his high-heeled boots. "Brand my prairie pork chops, what's goin' on here?" He took off his ten-gallon hat and scratched his bald head.

As the cook waited for an answer, the three youths stared at him in sheer dazzlement. Chow, who had a weakness for fancy Western shirts, had outdone himself.

"Quick! My sunglasses!" Bud gasped, shielding his eyes.

Chow's shirt was of a brilliant orange hue, and decorated in yellow and red. Over the shirt was a beaded buckskin vest.

"I reckoned this here fancy li'l number would catch your eye, but never mind tryin' to butter me up!" said Chow, who sincerely believed his shirts were admired by everyone. "What I want to know is, who spread the hogwash about Tom bein' all laid up with *ee*-lectric burns?"

"It's true, old-timer," said Tom. "I did get a bit scorched yesterday."

Chow looked at his young boss more closely. His face showed quick concern when he saw the reddened patches of skin left from yesterday's accident.

"The doctor just took off the dressings," Tom explained. "Whatever he put on really did the trick—everything healed up fine."

"I was sure worried plumb stiff!" the cook admitted. "Soon as I heard it, I rassled up some o' your favorite grub an' hopped the first plane comin' to the Citadel. But I'm sure glad you're better now."

"Thanks, Chow." Tom threw an arm warmly around the chef's shoulders and in a Texas drawl said, "I know I can always count on you when things go wrong, pardner. How about sashayin' over to the lab with us?"

"Sure thing, boss," Chow agreed, his leathery face breaking into a pleased smile.

Bud and Ted had driven to the infirmary in a jeep, but Tom vetoed this form of transportation to the laboratory. "Let's walk," he suggested. "I need to stretch my legs."

"Ought to keep a string o' saddle horses around here," Chow grumbled. "Feller might catch his boot heel in a prairie-dog hole!"

"Well, if you insist upon wearing shoes with heels like a woman's what do you expect?" Tom chuckled. "Come on. I know a short cut."

He led the way through a cluster of workshops and laboratory buildings, then headed across a bare expanse of sun-baked sand toward his private lab. Suddenly his companions were startled by a loud buzz.

"What's that?" Ted asked.

"My pocket radio," Tom explained. He pulled

out the tiny transistor set and clipped the receiver to his ear. "Tom Swift here."

The next instant Tom's face turned pale. "Run!" he yelled to the others.

Following Tom's command, his three friends broke into a headlong sprint, dashing with him toward the laboratory.

"What in tarnation's the idea?" Chow panted as he ran. "Walkin' ain't bad enough, so we got to race? I ain't no Texas quarter horse—!"

Tom and his friends were hurtled helter-skelter

His words were drowned out by a rumbling noise underfoot. Then the ground exploded beneath the group! Tom and his friends were hurtled helter-skelter amid a shower of sand, dirt, and flying rocks!

As the shock of the blast died away, scientists and crewmen came rushing from the nearby buildings. They ran to aid the four victims, who lay momentarily stunned. Fortunately, none of them had any serious injuries.

"Wow!" said Bud in a dazed voice, as someone helped him upright. "Am I still in one piece?"

"Must be," joked Chris Barlow, a reactor technician. "I don't see any loose fragments lying around."

Nearby, Dr. Arndt Henry, the chief atomic scientist at the Citadel, was apologizing to Tom.

amid a shower of sand and flying rocks

"Sorry, skipper, I should have warned you before-hand that this area was off limits. But I thought you were still in the infirmary. We were carrying out an underground test."

He now turned to the other boys and Chow. "Surely you saw the sign posted in your dorm?"

Sheepishly Bud confessed they had failed to read the bulletin board. Chow, having recently arrived, had not seen the notice.

"It sure has taught me a lesson," Bud remarked woefully.

"Come near bein' a short cut to the next world!" Chow grunted as he staggered to his feet.

Ted grinned wryly. "Guess we're tougher than we thought, fellows."

Reassured that no one was injured, the group dispersed. At the lab a few minutes later, Tom started to make preparations for a test of his mat-ter-making machine.

"Nice job you fellows did," he congratulated Bud and Ted after checking the cooling appara-tus for the aluminum bars.

"Maybe we'd better stand well back—just in case," Bud said half-jokingly.

"Suit yourself." Tom smiled. "Here goes!" He closed the switch, feeding power to the machine, and adjusted the control knobs.

There was a steady hum of current as the ma-chine throbbed into action. To everyone's relief, the cooling apparatus did its job effectively and the aluminum bars stood firm. Tom settled down to tending the dials in silent absorption. Bud,

Ted, and Chow watched in fascination as an hour, then another, went by. Finally, they left to attend to other tasks.

To everyone's amazement, Tom continued to run the machine throughout the night and into the next day. He broke off his vigil only long enough to eat a few bites of the hot, tempting food which Chow brought him at intervals.

It was late afternoon of the next day when Tom finally called a halt, after operating the machine to the limit of its capacity. Thirty hours had elapsed since the start of the test!

Bud, Chow, and Ted rejoined Tom and gathered around to watch in fascination as he drew off a tiny quantity of gas. He analyzed it in the Swift spectroscope, then measured its mass on a microbalance.

Bud saw the young inventor's face turn bleak. "Failure?" he asked.

Tom shook his head. "Not exactly, fellows. But . . ." His voice trailed off in discouragement.

CHAPTER V

EXCITING PLANS

"WHAT'S wrong, boss?" Chow anxiously asked Tom.

The young inventor smiled wanly. "A million watts of electrical energy! And all my invention produced was this measly amount of gas!"

"But the spectroscope shows that it's pure oxygen," Bud spoke up.

"Yes, which weighs up to exactly one one-thousandth of a gram!"

Chow pushed back his ten-gallon hat and scratched his balding head. "Reckon that ain't very much, eh?"

"About enough to keep a flea alive for half a second." Tom whipped out his slide rule and did some rapid figuring. "Chow, with the power I used to make this much oxygen, you could run your toaster an hour a day for eighty-one years!"

"Wal, brand my coyote cutlets!" Chow gulped. "I—uh—how—" he floundered, trying to think of some way to comfort his young boss, but words failed him. He glanced helplessly at Bud and Ted.

Bud broke the glum silence by clapping Tom on the back. "So what? Fleas need oxygen too, don't they? Cheer up, pal. At least your machine works!"

Tom chuckled good-naturedly. "Guess you're right at that, Bud. But this is only a start." He paced back and forth with his hands in the pockets of his slacks, then turned to face Bud and Ted. "It looks as if even the Citadel isn't the place to finish this experiment."

"Meaning what?" Ted asked.

"Meaning we'll rocket up to our space station and use solar radiation as our source of power."

Tom Swift's outpost in space was a huge, wheel-shaped satellite, orbiting 22,300 miles above the earth. Tom had designed it as a factory for charging his famous solar batteries, as well as a scientific observation post and TV relay station.

"Yip-pee!" Bud yelled, and swung his friend around the floor a couple of times.

"Put 'er there, skipper!" said Ted and pumped Tom's hand up and down.

"Hold it, fellows!" Tom spluttered with laughter. "This is serious business."

"Who said it wasn't?" retorted Bud cheerfully.

"I mean it," Tom insisted. "Look! Some day I hope to colonize the moon. A base there would yield all sorts of valuable data—not just about the moon itself, but the earth and the rest of the solar system."

"You mean through observations by telescope from a lunar observatory?" Ted asked.

"Exactly," Tom replied. "What's more, we might be able to mine valuable raw materials up there, such as that unknown hydrogen compound I picked up on our Swift spectroscope."

Tom had made this exciting discovery a few months before, when he had won a victory over his Brungarian rivals in making the first landing on the moon.

"However," Tom went on, "in order to set up a permanent base on the moon, we'll need a tremendous supply of oxygen, food, and water. And the only way I can see to accomplish that is by perfecting my matter-making machine."

"Wouldn't it be possible to grow plants on the moon to feed your lunar colony?" Ted asked.

Tom shook his head. "No, because on the moon you'd get two weeks of daylight, followed by two weeks of darkness. Plants couldn't survive under those conditions."

"How about growing them underground by artificial light?" Bud suggested.

"Too wasteful of energy," Tom pointed out. "Also, to feed even a few men, we'd need too large an area for raising the plants. And that's not even mentioning the extremes of heat and cold which would kill off most forms of plant life in short order."

"Okay, *I'm* convinced!" Bud exclaimed. "How soon do we start for the outpost?"

Tom smiled. "I want to discuss the whole project with Dad first. We'll start back to Shopton early tomorrow morning."

"Hold on now, boss," Chow spoke up plaintively. "You ain't said nothin' yet about *me* goin' along on this trail drive up yonder."

Bud pretended to look worried. "Old-timer, we weren't going to tell you the bad news just yet. But the fact is, crewmen with oversized bay windows won't qualify for any more space flights. The strain is too great."

"The strain is too great?" Chow snorted indignantly. "Why, brand my space boots, didn't I stand the strain all right when we built the space wheel and explored the satellite Little Luna and even flew clear up to the moon? Didn't crack up on any o' *them* space flights, did I?"

"Oh, I'm not worried about *you*," said Bud. "I mean the strain of the extra poundage might be too great on the spaceship."

A deep red flush spread over Chow's tanned features. "I can't help what my own cookin' does to me," he said. "Now can I, Tom?"

"Don't let Bud kid you, Chow," Tom said. "I wouldn't take off without my old pal any more than I'd take off without a space helmet. Why, a good space cook like you is the most important man in the crew!"

Chow grinned in relief and threw out his chest until he seemed in danger of popping a button.

"Thanks, boss. And as fer you, Buddy boy, don't come runnin' to ole Chow next time you get space sick. If you can't stand the gaff, we'll jest have to ship you straight back to earth!"

The session broke up in good-natured needling, and the following day Tom and his three companions took off for Shopton. A heavy overcast darkened the sky. Within an hour after leaving the Citadel, they saw lightning flashes arc through the clouds, while the heavens rumbled with thunder.

"Looks as if we're in for a rough flight," Ted remarked.

The words were hardly out of his mouth when terrific headwinds buffeted the plane. Splashes of rain pelted the cabin window as the storm unleashed its full fury below.

"I'd better take her upstairs," Tom said, hauling back on the stick. The big cargo jet zoomed upward in a steep climb. "Flick on the radio to Enterprises, will you?" he asked Bud.

The copilot tuned to the special frequency. "Swift jet calling Enterprises! Can you read me?"

The Enterprises operator responded, and a moment later switched the call to Mr. Swift in his private office.

"Hello, Bud! Is Tom aboard?"

"Yes, Mr. Swift. He's right here."

Tom used his throat mike. "Hi, Dad! How's everyone?"

"All fine, son, but we were a bit worried when we heard about you getting burned." Tom reassured his father and Mr. Swift went on, "How about your matter-making machine? Did the tests work out?"

"Well enough to prove my point," Tom replied. "But the power consumption is so high, I believe I'd better continue my experiments up at the space station." Tom waited for his father to comment, but the set remained silent. "Dad, are you there? Can you read me?"

Tom thumbed his mike switch and adjusted the tuning, but the radio seemed to have gone dead.

"What's wrong?" Bud shot a puzzled glance at the young pilot.

"Not sure," Tom replied, "but take a look at some of those dials."

"Jumpin' jets! The flight instruments have gone haywire too!"

Ted bent forward to look over Bud's shoulder.

"What caused it, skipper?"

Tom shook his head, a worried frown creasing his brow. "I don't know, but I have a hunch it may be due to sunspots."

Fortunately, the gyrocompass was not affected and the plane continued its steady flight above the storm area. After a moment's silence, Bud asked thoughtfully:

"Skipper, what would happen if we were up on the moon and depending on your matter maker for food and oxygen? Would sunspots throw *that* out of kilter too?"

"Brand my jet scooter," Chow burst out nervously, "why bring that up?"

Tom grinned at the apprehensive stares of his three friends. "Relax," he said. "It actually wouldn't make much difference. Might cut down on production a little, or even boost it a bit, but otherwise it wouldn't affect the machine at all."

Chow fanned himself with his ten-gallon hat. "Might 'a' knowed that Buddy boy was jest tryin' to spook us. Trouble with some hombres is they got too much *ee*-magination!"

Shortly before noon, the ship landed at Enterprises and Tom hurried to the big double office he shared with his father. Besides the huge modern desks for father and son, the room contained comfortable leather chairs, push-button drawing boards, and in front of one wall near the door a movable stack of shelves. They were crowded with books and shiny models of Tom Sr.'s and Tom Jr.'s greatest inventions, and also sample bottles of their various chemical compounds.

Over a tasty lunch of chicken sandwiches, Tom discussed with his father the new plans for experimenting with his matter-making machine at the outpost in space.

"I agree, son," the elder scientist nodded. "You apparently need the intense solar radiation you'll get above the earth's atmosphere to provide you with an unlimited source of power."

Mr. Swift broke off as the telephone rang. He lifted the receiver, spoke for a few minutes, then hung up with a chuckle.

"Better fit a dinner party this evening into your schedule," he told Tom. "That was Sandy. She has invited Phyl and wants you to bring Bud and Ted."

"We'll be there," Tom promised, grinning.

Phyllis Newton was Tom's favorite date. A pretty brunette, she was the daughter of "Uncle Ned" Newton, stanch and long-time friend of Mr. Swift. He was now manager of the Swift Construction Company. In their youth the two men had struggled side by side through many exciting adventures when Tom Sr. was first startling the world with his advanced scientific achievements.

That evening, the dining-room table in the Swift home looked unusually attractive, with flowers, silver, fine china, and candles. As Tom held his mother's chair, he asked, "Did I forget somebody's birthday?"

Sandy laughed. "No, but this is a special occasion."

"What are we celebrating?" Bud asked.

"Well," said Sandy, "Phyl and I decided to drum up a little excitement. You boys have all the fun on these space flights. Why not take *us* along? You could teach me to pilot the *Challenger,* Tom!"

"And I could be her back-seat driver!" added Phyl, her brown eyes twinkling.

The *Challenger,* Tom's amazing new spaceship powered by repelatron drive, had already successfully orbited the moon.

As Tom hesitated, his father spoke up. "That

might be a good idea. You could observe the feminine reaction to space travel." He chuckled. "I've heard they're better in their behavior than men."

"Oh, Dad, you're wonderful!" Sandy cried, popping up from her chair to give her father a hug. "Then it's all settled."

Dinner proceeded to the accompaniment of frequent laughter and banter among the Swifts and their guests. As they were eating dessert, apple pie à la mode, the phone rang and Sandy went to answer it.

"For you, Ted," she informed him.

Ted excused himself to take the call. When he returned to the table a few moments later, his face was very pale. The others noticed his concern with alarm.

"I do hope it wasn't bad news, Ted," Mrs. Swift said.

Ted shrugged uneasily as he resumed his place. "I'm not sure *how* to take it," he replied. "I've just been threatened!"

CHAPTER VI

A NIGHT OF PERIL

TED'S announcement brought gasps of dismay from his listeners.

"Who was it?" Tom questioned. "That Mr. Hampshire again?"

Ted shook his head. "This time the caller gave no name, but I'm sure the voice wasn't Hampshire's."

"What did he say?" Mr. Swift asked.

"He asked me if I was going to co-operate with Hampshire," Ted replied. "When I told him no, he became furious and said, 'If you don't, your life won't be worth a plugged nickel!'"

Bud broke the tense silence that followed. "Ted, it looks as if the only safe place for you will be the space outpost—or the moon!"

Mrs. Swift, with her usual motherly concern, had a more practical suggestion. "Ted, why not stay here for the time being? We have plenty of room, and you'll be protected by our warning system!"

This system, devised by Tom and his father,

47

maintained a magnetic field around the Swift house and grounds. Anyone entering the field, unless wearing a special deactivator mechanism, triggered off an alarm inside the house.

"That's very kind of you, Mrs. Swift," Ted replied, "but Mother and Ray may be in danger too. I wouldn't want to leave them alone."

"Before we decide anything," Tom put in, "let me call Harlan Ames. He was to be at the plant tonight."

Tom hurried to the Swifts' second telephone, a private wire to Enterprises. When the security chief heard what had happened, he suggested that Ted stay at Enterprises, which was guarded by a tight security setup, and that his family be flown by helicopter to Ames's private cottage on Blue-jay Lake.

"There's plenty of frozen and canned food there," he explained, "and they'll be perfectly safe. The spot is accessible only by plane."

"Good deal, Harlan!" Tom concurred. "Thanks a million."

Ted agreed at once to Ames's suggestion and suggested that he call his mother at once.

"Better not," Tom advised. "Hampshire and his gang may be tapping your phone. We'll pick up your mother and Ray by car and drive them to the Enterprises airfield."

It was decided as a safety measure to divide forces. Ted and Bud would go first in Bud's convertible, while Tom and Mr. Swift followed in Tom's sports car.

As they were about to leave, Mrs. Swift spoke nervously to her husband. "I—I don't want to seem unduly worried, my dear, but do you suppose someone might be watching the house right now? If so, he may trail you."

Mr. Swift gave her a reassuring hug. "You may have a point there, Mary—we'll check. Switch on all the yard lights, Tom."

"Right, Dad. I'll turn Caesar and Brutus loose, too. They'll certainly let us know if anyone's lurking around!"

The two bloodhounds were kenneled outside. Besides being the Swift family pets, they were also highly trained watchdogs.

Tom pressed a master switch, controlling a number of spotlights concealed in the shrubbery. Instantly the house and grounds were bathed in a brilliant radiance.

Then he and Bud hurried out to open the kennel. With eager yelps, the two bloodhounds came loping out. They ambled about, lifting their heads occasionally to sniff the night air, but gave no sign of detecting any unfamiliar scents.

"All clear," Tom reported. "Let's get going!"

The trip to Ted Spring's house was completed without incident. The others waited outside while Ted went in to tell his mother and brother about moving to Ames's cottage, and help pack for the trip. Tom had parked his low-slung sports car at the curb behind Bud's red convertible. Minutes later, Ted emerged from the house alone, looking anxious and worried.

"What about your mother and Ray?" asked Mr. Swift. "Nothing wrong, is there?"

"They won't come," Ted reported. "Mother says she feels safer right here in her own home."

"That's natural, I suppose," said Mr. Swift, "but in this case I strongly believe it would be better for her to follow our plan."

"I've tried to convince her, sir. Would you talk to her, please? I'm sure she'll listen to you."

Mr. Swift grinned sympathetically and opened the car door. "All right, son. I hope your confidence isn't misplaced, but I'll see what I can do."

While Mr. Swift and Ted went back inside, Tom and Bud scouted around cautiously for signs of anyone spying on the house. All seemed quiet and normal. The only other cars parked on the street were empty.

Fifteen minutes later Mrs. Spring and Ray came out, accompanied by Ted and Mr. Swift, who were carrying the suitcases. The boys loaded these into the convertible's trunk, then Tom assisted Mrs. Spring into the back seat. The slender, dark-haired woman wore an anxious, tense look.

"I do hope I've made the right decision," she fretted.

"I'm sure you have," said Tom reassuringly. "Believe me, you and Ray will be perfectly safe at Bluejay Lake."

"Sure we will," Ray spoke up stoutly. "Boy, it'll be fun going up there!" He climbed in beside her, and Ted took the front seat with Bud.

As the red convertible pulled away from the curb, Tom followed close behind with his father. Cutting straight across town, they took the road leading to Swift Enterprises, which lay on the outskirts of Shopton.

"Lights behind us, Dad," said Tom tersely, glancing at the rear-view mirror.

As Mr. Swift turned to look, the car approached rapidly, then swung to the left to pass. Hitting at least sixty miles an hour, the car roared alongside, then swung broadside into the path of Bud's convertible!

Bud slammed on the brakes. Too late! With a deafening impact of crumpling metal, the red convertible plowed into the sedan, which had stopped dead ahead.

"Great Scott!" gasped Mr. Swift in horror.

Only quick action on Tom's part prevented a second collision. The instant he brought his car to a halt, both he and his father leaped out to aid the others.

"Anyone hurt?" Tom cried, ripping open the door of the convertible.

There was silence for several seconds, then Bud replied woozily, "I'm okay, I guess."

"Me, too," Ted spoke up. "Banged my head pretty hard. Mother, Ray, are you—?"

Mrs. Spring and Ray reported being shaken up and bruised, but otherwise uninjured.

"Thank goodness," said Mr. Swift.

"But why did that driver ahead pull in front of

us?" Mrs. Spring asked. "And what happened to him?"

"He ran away," Ted answered. "He jumped out the instant he stopped. I saw him dart off the road to the right just before we crashed and our headlights went out."

"I'll bet it was Hampshire," Bud declared. "What did he look like?"

"I didn't see his face," Ted replied.

Tom got a powerful flashlight from the glove compartment of his own car and played it back and forth in the direction Ted had indicated. The area bordering the road was an open field which seemed to offer no hiding place.

"That's funny." Ted frowned. "I'm sure he headed over this way somewhere."

The driver of the sedan jumped ou

"It's possible," Tom pointed out, "that he started to the right just to mislead us, and then doubled back across the road later."

The left side was overgrown with trees and tangled underbrush.

"Wait here," Tom told the others. "There's probably not much chance of finding him, but I'll take a look."

Crossing the road, Tom moved cautiously among the trees, probing here and there with his flashlight. From time to time, he turned off the light and paused to listen for the sound of footsteps or other movements. Suddenly Tom froze in the darkness as his ears caught the murmur of voices.

"We've got the guy scared now," a man was saying. "Pretty soon, we should have our mitts on the Swifts' plans. Then we'll pass 'em along to the right party!"

and darted off into the woods

CHAPTER VII

ANTITRUTH SERUM

TOM repressed a surge of anger and focused his attention on locating the men, whose voices he did not recognize. Where were they?

Tom swung his light in all directions. But the yellow beam revealed nothing except tree trunks and gloomy undergrowth. Suddenly he realized that he was making a target of himself.

"Oh—oh! Those fellows may be armed!" he reflected, snapping off the flashlight hastily.

But how to find them in the darkness? Scarcely a ray of moonlight penetrated through the leafy branches overhead. Then a plan occurred to Tom —an old trick which might fool his unseen enemies. He jammed his flashlight into the crotch of a tree and turned on the beam again. Then, moving silently as an Indian, he began picking his way toward the voices.

To Tom's annoyance, the men had stopped talking. His keen senses enabled him, however, to hazard a guess as to their possible location.

Tom was hoping they might launch an attack of some kind toward the flashlight and thus give themselves away.

So far, they had shown no sign of rising to the bait. The silence continued, broken only by the chirp of crickets and other night noises.

Step by step, Tom silently inched his way forward. To his chagrin, his efforts proved fruitless. Broken underbrush showed where the men had been crouching.

"Have they ducked out of sight temporarily?" Tom asked himself. "What if they circle behind me, waiting for a chance to strike?" The thought made the hairs bristle at the nape of Tom's neck!

Suddenly, from the road, came the sound of a car starting up. Galvanized into action, Tom rushed toward the highway. He was just in time to see a sedan without lights pull out from among the trees and roar off into the darkness. Thoroughly disgusted, he retraced his steps toward the scene of the crash.

"Tough luck," Bud greeted him. "We heard the getaway car."

Tom nodded gloomily. "Apparently our little pal had a friend waiting for him—with transportation." He reported the conversation which he had overheard in the woods.

"Someone's sure out to make trouble for you Swifts," Bud said worriedly to Tom and his father.

Mr. Swift nodded, frowning. "And so far, no clues to his—or their—identity." To Tom he added, "The car's ten years old. Not much loss. No license plates and no serial numbers, either. We checked, but they've been filed off, so these men must have been planning an accident like this for some time. I've radioed the police, by the way."

Mrs. Spring, who had been trying to remain calm, now said with a tremble in her voice, "Oh, dear, I *knew* we should have stayed home."

At that moment everyone's attention was diverted by the siren of the approaching police car. A moment later it pulled up behind them with a screech of brakes. Four officers piled out.

"Mr. Swift?"

"Right here," said the scientist. "But there's no use searching for the car owner here. He just got away with the aid of a confederate."

Tom gave the sergeant in charge a meager description of the getaway car, remarking that he thought from the sound of the motor it was a two-year-old Renser. Meanwhile, another officer was radioing word to additional scout cars, as well as to the state police.

"We'll have all roads blocked," the sergeant said. "With luck, we may still pick those men up. We'll have the wrecked car towed off and keep it for evidence."

Fortunately, in spite of a crumpled front end, leaking radiator and no lights, Bud's convertible was still in operating condition.

"It'll get us to Enterprises, if the police will let me follow you, Tom," he said. After getting the sergeant's permission, he cried, "Let's go!"

In a few minutes they arrived at the experimental station and drove to the airstrip where a helicopter was warmed up and waiting.

"Now don't worry," Ted soothed his mother. "You're doing the right thing."

"All right, Teddy." She sighed, giving him a kiss on the cheek. "But do take care of yourself."

"And I'll take care of Mom!" Ray promised.

"That's the spirit!" Tom said, as the youngster shook hands with everyone.

The two passengers were helped aboard the helicopter—Ray filled with excitement at his first whirlybird flight. Moments later, the craft soared aloft and disappeared northward into the night sky.

"Guess I'll have to leave my car here overnight till I get that radiator fixed," Bud remarked. "She's leaking fast."

"Stick around and keep me company," Ted invited. "Tom has assigned me to one of the guest suites reserved for VIP's."

These were rooms on an upper floor of the Enterprises main building, set aside for the use of government officials and distinguished scientists who often visited the experimental station.

"I'll accept." Bud grinned.

"It might be a good idea to have Doc Simpson check you boys and put something on Ted's forehead. You really have a goose egg there," Mr. Swift said.

Tom and his father took the boys to the plant

infirmary in the sports car and went inside with them. As Doc Simpson, the Enterprises young physician, made his examinations, he listened to their account of the night's adventure and their suspicion that Hampshire might be the instigator of the accident.

"In case there's any danger that one of you might fall into the hands of this fellow Hampshire or whoever's behind this rough stuff," Doc said, "it might be wise to take precautions."

"Do you have something special in mind?" Mr. Swift asked.

"Yes. As you know, there are certain drugs which can be given to make a person talk, even against his will," Doc Simpson began. "We call them truth serums. Now, if Hampshire or someone else did capture one of you, he might administer such a drug to force you to reveal your secret plans."

"That's so," agreed Mr. Swift thoughtfully. "If they learned the details of Tom's space projects, it could even endanger our national security."

"All the more reason to take no chances," Doc urged. "I've been developing a serum to counteract such 'truth' drugs. If you like, I could give you all a shot of it right now."

"An *anti*truth serum?" said Tom. "Dad, I think that's a good suggestion."

Mr. Swift agreed, as did Bud and Ted, so all four bared their arms. A nurse swabbed their skin with alcohol, and Doc Simpson then administered the serum to each one by hypodermic needle.

"Boy, we didn't know what we were getting into." Bud grinned as he rolled down his shirt sleeve. "Next time, I'll keep my bumps to myself!"

Tom chuckled. "Remember, it's all in the cause of science!"

After exchanging good-nights, Bud and Ted retired to the Enterprises guest room, while Tom and his father drove home. Reaching it, the Swifts retired at once. Tom fell asleep almost as soon as his head touched the pillow.

It seemed only minutes later when the young inventor was awakened by the loud ringing of his bedside telephone. Tom groped sleepily for the instrument and glanced at the radium dial of his wrist watch.

"Twenty past midnight!" he groaned inwardly. "Hello—Tom Swift Jr. speaking."

A man's muffled voice spoke. "Don't think you've fooled us, Swift. The Springs ain't safe— or you and your family either!"

"Who is this?" Tom snapped, now thoroughly awake. He was trying to figure out if the speaker was one of the men he had overheard in the woods.

But the receiver had already clicked at the other end of the line. Realizing there was little chance of tracing the call, Tom hung up. He lay awake for nearly an hour, mulling over the threat. There was no question now but that he as well as Ted had become involved in some mysterious plot.

"But what exactly is the reason?" he kept asking himself. "The publication of the *Journal?* There must be more to it than that."

Next morning he reported the matter at once to the security department. "I don't like this," said Ames. "For Pete's sake, Tom, watch your step."

On the way to the laboratory, Tom was hailed for a conference with his father on the technical papers for the *Enterprises Journal.*

"Looks like a swell first issue, Dad," Tom remarked enthusiastically.

"Yes indeed, son," said Mr. Swift. "I think we can all be proud of it. You know, Tom, this has been a dream of mine ever since we founded Swift Enterprises. I look forward to the day when scientists all over the world can exchange their findings freely for the good of mankind."

Tom, too, cherished the same dream. "I'm sure that day will come, Dad," he asserted.

Gathering up the papers, he turned them over to a young secretary to be taken to the printer. Miss Warner was substituting for the vacationing regular secretary, Miss Trent.

Tom now phoned Arv Hanson, asking him to come to the office. Arv, a hulking six-footer, was the Swifts' chief modelmaking engineer. A fine precision craftsman, Arv turned out the delicately tooled models of all the Swifts' major inventions.

One example of his handiwork, standing on Tom's desk, was a blue plastic model of the young inventor's jetmarine. Another was a small silvery replica of the *Star Spear,* Tom's first rocket ship.

"What cooks, skipper?" asked Arv as he walked in.

"Special job I'd like you to handle," Tom replied. "Sit down, Arv."

He briefed the engineer on his matter-making machine, telling of the need for a tremendous supply of energy to operate it. "For the time being, I'll carry on my experiments at the space station," Tom went on, "using a solar-battery setup. But for full-time operation aboard a spaceship or on the moon, I'll need a much better method of power supply."

"What do you have in mind?" Arv asked.

"A device which you might call a 'power gatherer' or 'energy collector,' " Tom said. "Each collector will be a huge sheet about four acres in size. The ship will carry a dozen or more of them."

"Four *acres!*" Arv gasped. "How do you expect to load them aboard the spaceship?"

"Each one will be made up of small squares, so that it can be folded into a compact bundle," Tom explained. "The squares will be held together by a framework of foil tubing. When we're out in space, helium gas will be pumped into the tubing. This will cause the whole sheet to open up to its full size outside the ship, just like one of those paper snakes you blow into at kids' parties."

"I get it." Arv nodded. "And there's no air drag in space, so it'll be no problem to *keep* the sheets flattened out."

"Right," said Tom. "Now, each of the small squares in the sheet will be made up of twin leaves of Tomasite plastic—one with luxium metal, and the other with conductate metal."

The two amazing metal alloys had been developed by Tom for his spaceship's energy-conversion units on his first trip to the moon. When placed in contact with each other and exposed to sunlight, the two metals formed a cell which generated an electric current.

"How do we stamp the luxium and conductate on the plastic leaves?" asked Arv.

Tom explained that each pair of leaves would bear a number of tiny cells laid out in "dot-and-dash" pattern. The pattern for each leaf would first be photographed from a drawing, then printed in varnish on the metal-coated plastic. The leaf would then be soaked in a chemical bath, leaving only the dot-and-dash pattern of metal on the plastic.

"One leaf would have the luxium pattern, and the other leaf would have the conductate pattern," Tom went on, sketching out each pattern in pencil. "So when we press the two leaves together, they'll form a powerful compound electric cell."

"And your energy collector will have a whole flock of these twin-leaf cells, supported by a framework of foil tubing," Arv concluded.

"Exactly. It should generate an enormous flow of current."

Arv scratched his head. "Sounds like quite a job, skipper."

Tom grinned. "I'm sure you can handle it."

"It's an amazing idea," commented Mr. Swift, who had listened with keen attention to his son's explanation. "I think it should solve your problem, Tom. And also—"

Crash!

All three looked up to see a cascade of bottles and models tumbling from the case of shelves near the door. At almost the same instant the office door slammed shut.

"Someone was hiding behind those shelves!" Tom cried out. "And listening to every word we said!"

CHAPTER VIII

SPACE OUTPOST

JUMPING up from their chairs, Tom, Arv, and Mr. Swift rushed out to the corridor. But there was no sign of the mysterious eavesdropper.

"He must have sneaked in here and overheard the plans for your energy collectors!" Arv said uneasily.

Tom nodded, his face grim. "And he also must be an employee of Swift Enterprises."

Tom and his father exchanged worried glances. It was an unpleasant thought that some trusted worker might be a spy. Yet no outsider could have slipped in past the tight security setup which ringed the experimental station.

"I'll call Security and ask Ames to make a check," said Mr. Swift, returning to the office.

Meanwhile, a number of people who had heard the crash had run out of adjoining offices into the corridor to see what was happening. They milled around asking questions, but Tom quieted them with a few smiling remarks.

As the crowd dispersed, Tom noticed one young man whom he had never seen before, with sandy hair and a rather full face.

"Who's that?" he whispered, nudging Arv Hanson.

Arv grinned. "His name's Amberson Lintner —Amby for short. Just out of engineering college. Confidentially, he's been dating your temporary secretary."

"What does he do here?" Tom asked.

Arv shrugged. "Oh, he's taking the training program. Spends time in every department. He'd like to be a big shot, but I doubt if he'll make the grade."

"How come?"

"Too much of a talker. Smart enough but lets everybody know it."

Two days later, after making preparations for the trip to the space outpost, Tom, Bud, Ted, and Mr. Swift flew to Fearing Island for the take-off. The other passengers for the trip included Sandy, Phyl, Chow Winkler, and Doc Simpson.

Fearing Island, the Swifts' rocket research base, was a thumb-shaped stretch of sand dunes and scrubgrass. It lay not far off the Atlantic coast and was guarded by drone planes and radar.

From the island airfield, the travelers drove to the special launching area for the *Challenger*. Here the great silver spaceship, already checked and loaded for flight, stood glistening in the morning sunshine.

"Just think," murmured Phyl, gazing in awe at

the powerful craft, "the *Challenger* has actually been to the moon!"

Bud added proudly, "She may not look very streamlined, but this baby can travel like a comet!"

The huge boxlike cabin, poised on four hydraulic landing struts, was encircled by a framework of slender rails for the swiveling radiator antennas which beamed out the repelatron force rays.

Although the ship had auxiliary rockets for emergency maneuvering, its main motive power was the repelatron drive. This drive system could be used to propel the ship in any direction by exerting a repulsion force against the earth, moon, or any heavenly object.

"All aboard!" Tom called, after a last-minute check with the mechanics and ground crew.

One by one, passengers and crew trooped up the accommodation ladder to the landing platform which projected from the front of the cabin. The landing platform was used for small auxiliary craft which could be berthed in the ship's hangar compartment.

Entering through an air lock, the space voyagers zoomed upward by elevator to the flight deck. Here a pair of bucket seats for the pilot and co-pilot stood in front of twin quartz-glass view windows. There were also seats for passengers and observers.

"Jeepers!" Sandy gasped. "Just *looking* at all those dials and control levers gives me a thrill.

Tom, do you think I can learn to fly this ship?"

"Sure you can, Sis." Tom grinned. "No work at all. Actually, the real work of flight control is done by electronic brains in the computer room."

"I'm glad we don't have to be strapped down on acceleration cots," Phyl remarked. "That's what scares *me* about rocket ships—the awful shock at blast-off."

"On this ship you can relax in perfect ease," Tom assured her. "The repelatron force rays apply a smooth flow of power so we can accelerate gradually, instead of in a few terrific bursts."

A warning buzzer sounded, and everyone took his seat. The voice of George Dilling, radio chief at Fearing, crackled over the speaker:

"All clear, skipper. Have a good trip!"

"Thanks, George," Tom replied. "Hold down the island!"

Outside, through the quartz-glass window, the ground crew chief gave the signal for take-off. Tom switched on the repelatron circuits, and a number of colored lights flashed on the element selector panel above the view panes.

"Watch those lights, Sis," Tom told Sandy. "They indicate the chemical make-up of the object we have to repel—in this case, the ground just below us. The repelatron circuits must respond to the exact radiation frequency of each element present."

As he spoke, Tom's hands flew busily over the controls. "What I'm doing now," he added, "is a sort of fine-tuning job to make sure we're adjusted not only for the right elements, but the right isotope of each element."

With the proper controls adjusted, Tom swiveled the radiator antennas into position for ground thrust and fed power to the repelatrons. Like a silver asteroid, the *Challenger* soared upward into the blue!

"This is known as a bouncing-ball take-off," Bud wisecracked to the girls.

"Seriously, that's just about what happens," Tom added. "The repelatron force rays push us away from the earth—or whatever object we aim at—just like a ball on the rebound."

As the earth fell away below them, the passengers crowded to the view windows. Fearing Island was a mere speck on the blue-green waters of the ocean. Through the low-lying blankets of mist, every detail of the Atlantic coast line was revealed.

"Tom, it's amazing to think how far science has progressed," said Mr. Swift gravely. "Not so long ago, people laughed at the possibility of space flight, and who knows what marvels lie ahead!"

Soon the roundness of the earth began to show in the curvature of the horizon. Off to the east, the travelers could make out the shore lines of Europe.

"An angel's-eye view!" murmured Phyl.

With the earth left well behind, Tom set a steady course for the space station, then lounged back in his pilot's seat. "Look! No hands!" He chuckled.

"Why, it's flying itself!" Sandy exclaimed. "Tom, this ship's a dream!"

"Shucks, you ain't seen nothin'!" Chow bragged. "Jest wait'll you see how I scoot around up here in my li'l ole jet-propelled space suit!"

"Why bother with a space suit!" Bud needled him. "We've been expecting you to take off in that shirt you're wearing!"

Chow preened himself proudly as the others stifled their amusement. His latest cowboy shirt was patterned with a wild galaxy of stars and planets. "I designed this here number myself, buckaroo. You couldn't buy another one like it fer love or money!"

"That I can believe," Bud muttered.

As they cruised silently upward beyond the earth's atmosphere, Tom checked out Sandy and Ted on the *Challenger's* controls.

"What's this on your left?" asked Ted, pointing to a large fluorescent screen.

"Our space position finder," Tom explained. He flicked a switch. As the screen lighted up, a large curved reddish area appeared with a small white dot close by. "The red area represents the earth, and the white dot is the space station. Farther out in space, the scope would pick up other objects in the solar system."

Tom also showed them a large control board which projected out on the right-hand side of the flight compartment. Its various dials were labeled for earth, moon, sun, Mars, Venus, and other heavenly bodies.

"The dials are fed by tapes from our electronic computers," Tom explained. "They tell us the distance and angle of each body from our spaceship, and how much force we need to repel them for any desired acceleration."

"Skipper, if I needed anything to prove you're a young genius, this is it," Ted said, wide-eyed with amazement.

"Take a bow, pal!" Bud grinned at Tom.

Soon the outpost in space loomed into view. Ted and the girls, who had never before visited the space station, gasped at the breath-taking spectacle.

The gigantic, silver-colored, wheel-shaped satellite, although seemingly motionless, spun in its orbit at 6,888 miles per hour. Antennas, polished reflectors, and a latticework telescope poked out from the twelve-spoked wheel.

"Each spoke is a separate unit," Tom explained to Ted. "Some are designed for crew's quarters or laboratories, one is an astronomical observatory, and others are assembly lines for charging solar batteries. Those polished reflectors are to focus the sunlight in on—"

Bud suddenly interrupted. "Skipper! The repelatron beamed at the earth won't turn off!"

Tom checked the controls hastily. He flicked several levers and switches without result.

"Something wrong, son?" asked Mr. Swift, stepping forward quietly.

"I can't decrease the earth force, Dad."

By this time, the ship appeared to be rushing

toward the space wheel at terrifying speed. In a matter of moments, they would crash!

"Gallopin' hoot owls!" Chow gulped, turning pale. "Can't you back up this here flyin' buckboard nohow?"

"Not exactly, but you've got the right idea, Chow," Tom gritted as his strong fingers moved rapidly over the control panel. "I'll aim the other repelatrons at the space wheel and try to avoid a crash," Tom said.

The passengers watched tensely as the ship gradually slowed into stable orbit close to the space station—its earth thrust neutralized by the forward repulsion rays.

"Quick thinking, Tom!" Mr. Swift congratulated his son.

"B-but how do we get over to the space station?" asked Phyl nervously.

"This is where Chow does that Daring-Young-Man-on-the-Jet-Propelled-Trapeze act he was telling you about." Bud grinned. "Into your space suits, me hearties!"

Normally the ship would have been locked to the space wheel by magnetic grapples, so that its passengers could step directly into the station's air lock. Now, however, the transfer would have to be made through the space void.

While rocket-propelled mooring cables were shot across to the station, everyone except Tom and Mr. Swift donned their space suits, boots, and helmets. One by one, they went out through the ship's air lock.

To allay the girls' nervousness, Bud went first to guide them across.

"Oh, boy! It's like stepping out into nothingness!" Phyl quavered over her suit radio.

Bud said reassuringly, "Just hang onto this cable at all times, and work your way across hand over hand. If that's too slow, you can trigger the jet pistol on your suit."

"No thanks. We'll do it the hard way," Sandy joked.

Chow, who was last, suddenly found he could not budge from the ship.

"Help! I'm stuck!" he yelped. "The force ray's got me!"

Hearing Chow's cry over his suit radio, Bud looked back. He was aghast to see that a leg of the Texan's pants was caught in the air lock. The copilot instantly realized that if Chow tried to wrench himself loose, the material might rip. Immediate depressurization would follow, then death!

"Chow! Your suit's caught. Don't move a muscle!" Bud hastily warned him, then radioed Tom to release the door mechanism.

It opened and Chow gingerly pulled himself free. "Buddy boy," he said, "you're a real friend. Closer'n a thistle burr. Thanks."

Soon, he, as well as the girls and the crew, were safely inside the station. Then Bud returned to help Tom and Mr. Swift, who were busy below decks in the compartment which housed the repelatron gear.

*To avoid a crash, Tom aimed the repelatrons
at the space wheel*

"Found the trouble yet?" Bud asked.

"It's the homing device that locks the main radiator on target," Tom replied, brushing the sweat from his eyes. "Somehow the circuit's jammed, so that it keeps feeding power and won't respond to the directional signal."

For a while the two scientists feared that it might be necessary to disconnect the homing device completely and resort to manual control. But at last, after several hours of work, Tom managed to correct the difficulty.

When father and son finally entered the space station, they were greeted by Ken Horton, commander of the outpost, a slender man of about thirty, with dark, close-cropped hair.

"Welcome, strangers!" he greeted them, shaking hands with the Swifts. "Tom, I'm eager to hear about this matter-making machine of yours."

A former Signal Corps officer, Horton had become the Swifts' first space trainee and had helped to build the station.

"The machine's still experimental, Ken," Tom replied. "I'm hoping to perfect it up here."

At that moment Bud nudged Tom and pointed to Ted Spring with a worried look. The young cadet was slumped on a bench in a hopeless, dejected attitude.

Tom felt a pang of fear. Had Ted succumbed to the dreaded "space sickness" which often struck new recruits on their first trip into the void?

CHAPTER IX

BLACKOUT!

STEPPING over to the young cadet, Tom laid a hand gently on his shoulder. "Feel all right, Ted?" he asked.

Ted looked up, forcing a smile. "Sure, skipper. I-I'm just a bit worried about my folks, that's all. Haven't heard a word from them since they left Shopton."

"We'll check right now," Tom promised. "Come with me."

Leading the way into the communications compartment, he asked the radio operator to contact Harlan Ames at Enterprises. A few moments later the security chief's voice came over the set:

"What's up, skipper?"

"Ted's worried about his mother and Ray," Tom explained. "Have you heard anything from them since they left Shopton?" he asked, as Ted bent forward to catch the answer.

"I talked to Mrs. Spring last night," Ames reported. "She said she'd just had another phone call from Hampshire."

"From Hampshire?" Ted broke in anxiously. "But how did he find out she was there?"

"Frankly, I don't know," Ames admitted. "Maybe from that same spy who sneaked into Tom's office. So far I haven't spotted him."

"What did Hampshire say?" Ted asked.

"He made no threats," Ames answered. "Just laughed about how we'd failed to outwit him. He said to Mrs. Spring, 'Here I am trying to do you a favor, and you run away from me!'"

Tom and Ted were startled. "Do you think that they're in any danger?" Tom asked Ames.

"Definitely not," the security man replied. "I had two guards fly up there this morning. The men are in constant touch with us here at the plant. As I told you, there are no motor roads leading to Bluejay Lake—and if any unidentified plane should appear, the guards will notify us at once."

Ted brightened immediately when he heard these arrangements. After sending a message to be relayed to his mother and Ray, the two youths signed off. "I'd give a lot to know how Hampshire got Mother's phone number," said Ted.

"It's just possible he made a wild guess," Tom suggested. "He may know of the secluded cottage and figured it's a good hiding place just as Ames did."

As the boys left the radio compartment, Ted

asked, "What's the first step on your program, Tom?"

"To assemble my matter-making machine and run off another test."

The various parts and subassemblies of the machine had already been unloaded from the *Challenger*. With the help of Ted and Bud, Tom set them up in his private laboratory, which occupied one whole spoke of the space wheel.

"How about your power hookup?" Bud asked.

"I'll use a bank of solar batteries," Tom said. "They'll stay right on the line so the sun's rays will be constantly recharging them."

Within an hour, the matter-making machine was ready to operate. Sandy and Phyl and Mr. Swift came to watch as Tom closed the main switch. With a loud hum, the current throbbed into action. Tom grinned as he saw the needle swing upward on the main ammeter.

"Good?" asked Sandy.

"Very good!" Tom replied. "This setup gives me much more current than I had at the Citadel."

Soon he was able to draw off a steady flow of gas from the machine. "Pure oxygen—and plenty of it!" Tom exulted, after testing the gas with a Swift spectroscope. "I think this machine is ready for a tryout on the *Challenger!*"

"Wonderful!" exclaimed Phyl, looking at Tom proudly.

"Amazing!" was Mr. Swift's verdict. "If the

machine works this well aboard the *Challenger,* you should be able to undertake any sort of space expedition."

Sandy smiled affectionately at her brother. "I knew you could do it. Have you named the new machine yet?"

Tom shook his head. "You give it one."

"How about space solartron?" Sandy suggested.

"Um, that sounds good," Tom mused.

"It's much better than matter maker," Phyl declared. "I suppose it means 'maker of matter through energy gathered in space from the sun.' "

Tom laughed. "You couldn't be more right, Phyl. And from now on it's the space solartron."

Bud spoke up. "Living in space seems to have improved Sandy's brain. Maybe you'd better not go home again." He closed his eyes and shielded them with one arm to shut out the withering look he received from Sandy.

After Tom and several of the men had disassembled the machine again, Tom supervised the job of setting it up aboard the spaceship. "We'll connect the output pipe directly to the ship's air-conditioning system," he told Bud and Ted.

This time, the electric current to operate the solartron would be drawn from the ship's powerful energy-conversion cells. These cells produced electricity by photochemical action of the sun's rays which were gathered and focused by dish-shaped reflectors mounted on the spaceship's cabin.

Bud and Ted were to be Tom's only companions for this first test cruise. "Good luck!" the girls radioed from the space station, as the young inventor prepared to take off.

"Thanks!" Tom replied into the mike. "Keep your fingers crossed, and maybe we'll bring you back some stardust!"

He switched on the repelatrons, released the magnetic grapples, and sent the *Challenger* zooming off in an orbit far above the space wheel.

"Ready, pals?" Tom asked. "Here's where we give the new machine the acid test."

He warmed up the solartron, turned off the regular air supply, and flipped a switch to feed oxygen from the machine into the ship's air-conditioning system. Several moments went by as the boys waited, a trifle nervously. Would the machine fail and their oxygen supply be completely cut off?

Finally Bud relaxed and slapped Tom on the back. "Well, we're still breathing." He chuckled. "Chum, it looks as though your machine's making the grade!"

Thrilled with excitement, Tom turned the controls over to Bud and went into the adjoining starboard compartment which contained the ship's pumping and air-conditioning equipment. Here he checked the various dials and valves on his matter-making machine. His new invention seemed to be working perfectly.

"With luck, we can plant a colony on the moon within a year!" Tom thought as he returned to the flight compartment.

"Must be good news from that look on your face," Ted remarked, grinning.

"It is." Tom grinned back. "If my first solartron can make oxygen this well, my next model should be able to produce anything we need for an extended space voyage!"

For over an hour the travelers cruised the space lanes, meanwhile eating the sandwiches and cocoa which Chow had prepared for them.

"Guess we may as well go back, fellows," Tom decided at last, satisfied with the results so far.

Neither of his companions replied. Surprised, Tom glanced at them, and noticed for the first time that both appeared drowsy. Bud was slumped in the copilot's seat, apparently almost half asleep.

"Hey, fly boy! Wake up!" Tom gave him a gentle shake.

To his amazement, the copilot's head lolled back. Bud's eyes flickered queerly and his breathing seemed heavy and labored. As Tom stared at him, he heard a loud *thump*. Springing up from his seat and whirling around, he saw that Ted had collapsed on the deck!

"What's wrong?" Tom gasped. He moved to assist Ted and discovered to his horror that his own legs felt weak!

After staggering a few steps, Tom had to lean against the bulkhead to support himself. His head was spinning and he felt slightly nauseated. Something must be wrong with the oxygen supply!

"I— I'd better switch to the regular system,"

Tom muttered. But his words trailed off. He seemed overcome by an urge to sleep. As he reached for the air-conditioning switch, he slid to the deck in an unconscious heap!

Some time later, Tom was awakened by a loud voice crackling over the radio. He was still too groggy to make out the words. By the time he gathered his wits, the voice had ceased.

"Where am I?" he wondered. Gradually he remembered how both his companions had lost consciousness. "I must have blacked out too!"

With a tremendous effort of will, he struggled to his feet and looked at the switch for the air-conditioning system. He had managed to turn it on part way. Now he flicked it to maximum. Then he got water from the scuttle butt and ammonia smelling salts from the first-aid locker. He went to work on Bud and Ted.

As the moments went by, Tom's head cleared. Soon his two companions regained consciousness.

"W-what happened?" Ted murmured groggily.

"Not sure yet," Tom replied, "but I suspect something went wrong with the solartron's oxygen supply. Here—drink some more of this water."

As soon as Bud and Ted were back on their feet, Tom hurried to check his matter-making machine. When he returned to the flight compartment, Bud flashed him a questioning glance.

"Figured it out yet?"

Tom nodded grimly. "According to the spectroscope, the machine was producing a one-hundred-thousandth of one per cent of carbon mon-oxide. Not fatal, but enough to knock us out!"

After radioing word to Horton and Mr. Swift, who had been calling them frantically, the boys returned to the space wheel.

"Oh, I'm so glad you're all right! You had us terribly worried," Phyl greeted them.

"Slight foul-up on my space solartron," Tom replied. He gave his father a complete report and added, "The machine was operating slightly off frequency, but I believe I've corrected the circuit design so it can't happen again."

To lighten the boys' spirits, Sandy put in teas-ingly, "Where's that stardust you promised us?"

"Have to take a rain check on that, Sis," Tom replied with a wry grin.

"Speaking of stardust," Mr. Swift remarked, "I'm engaged on a rather interesting experiment myself with cosmic dust."

The boys, who had known Mr. Swift was work-ing on a mysterious project of his own, were ea-ger to hear more. The scientist explained that he was developing a plan to fuse the tiny particles of cosmic dust in space into a mass large enough to form an "island in the sky."

"If my plan works," he told the others, "it will enable us to form space platforms or aster-oids anywhere in the solar system."

"What a setup!" Bud burst out. "Why, with space islands like that, we could set up way sta-tions en route to every planet!"

"Exactly." Mr. Swift nodded. "Even more important, the technique would give our country a most valuable means of controlling space in the interests of peace."

"You're right, Dad," said Tom, deeply impressed. "That's the most important goal we can aim for."

During the next two days, Tom began work on his second matter maker. Besides being much more powerful and efficient than his first machine, the new model would be able to produce many other elements besides oxygen.

"How soon will it be finished?" asked Sandy eagerly, as she watched her brother wire the electronic control panel.

Before answering, Tom ran off a quick series of calculations on one of his amazing miniature computers which Bud had dubbed "Little Idiots." Then he jotted down a correction on his blueprints.

"The design's complete right now, Sis," he replied. "However, the castings and some of the larger parts will have to be made back at Enterprises. The energy collectors to provide power for the machine are being made there, too."

"That means we go back to Shopton?" put in Bud.

Tom nodded. "The girls and you and I leave tomorrow. I'll radio ahead so work can be started on these other parts immediately. The blueprints can be televised."

Next day, the four young people took off in the *Challenger*. "Too bad we have to leave all those handsome outpost engineers behind." Sandy sighed and gave Phyl a mischievous twinkle.

Bud winked at Tom. "Lucky thing we're taking the girls home, skipper, before they get spoiled completely."

Tom chuckled. "Good idea for us to see that they get their feet back on the ground!"

As soon as the *Challenger* landed, Tom and his friends took off for Shopton. The young inventor hurried to consult Arv Hanson about progress on the energy collectors.

Arv shook his head grimly. "Sorry, skipper, we've had bad luck. The printing plates we made for the luxium and conductate leaves were mysteriously damaged. It may have been sabotage!"

CHAPTER X

LARIAT LIFELINE

TOM was startled. "Did you report the damaged plates to Harlan Ames?"

"Sure," Arv replied. "Security got on the job right away. They dusted the cracked plates for fingerprints, but there were none. Evidently the plates had been knocked off a shelf. They were badly scratched and marred. Security also looked for fingerprints in the whole working area, but all they found were mine and those of the other fellows assisting me on the job."

"Then there are no clues?" Tom asked.

Arv hesitated. "Well, Amby Lintner suggested one possible explanation."

"Lintner?" Tom was surprised. "He's not working on this project, is he?"

"No, but he pointed out that Bob Dowell had brought his dog into the photographic lab the day it happened. Bob wanted to use him as a subject for some high-speed camera experiments.

Amby said the dog may have broken loose and knocked the plates down."

"What do *you* think?" Tom asked.

Arv Hanson shrugged. "Bob says the dog was never out of his sight and that Amby's just trying to make himself look smart. I suppose it could have happened, though."

Tom frowned thoughtfully, remembering the mysterious eavesdropper who had knocked over the bottles in his office. Could it be that the same person was responsible for both accidents?

"Oh, well," he decided finally, "we can't let the accident stop us. Get busy on some new plates, will you, Arv?"

"We're already working on them, Tom," Hanson reported. "We'll rush the job through as fast as we can, but it'll probably be a couple of days before the sheets are ready."

"Okay, do the best you can."

At lunchtime in the company cafeteria, Tom related the incident to Bud.

"Does that mean your work is stalled until the energy collectors are ready?" Bud asked.

Tom shook his head as he spooned up the last of his oyster stew. "No, I'll go back up to the outpost and finish work on my second machine. I believe I can rig up a temporary power device. Want to come along?"

"Try to leave me behind!"

By midafternoon, the castings and other parts which Tom had requested by radio were finished. These were loaded aboard a cargo jet which Tom piloted to Fearing Island. From here, he and Bud blasted off in the *Challenger* for the return trip to the space station. They reached it on schedule.

After a few hours' rest, Tom plunged into work on the second model of his space solartron. In three hours it was assembled and ready for testing. The huge machine took up most of the available room in Tom's space laboratory, and the dial-studded control panel stood head-high to the two boys.

"Wow! What a monster!" Bud gasped. "You figure this will make other elements besides oxygen?"

"It should if I've designed it properly," said Tom. "See those push buttons marked *Element Control* and *Isotope Control?*"

Bud nodded. "What are they for?"

"By altering the velocity of the speeded-up particles, these control buttons will enable us to select any element—or any isotope of an element —that we want to produce," Tom explained. "Solid matter will be condensed in this receiving tank, after passing through the heat exchanger. And gases or liquids can be drawn off through this valve."

Bud scratched his head. "Looks as though it'll take enough power to drive a spaceship! Have you rigged up that temporary power source you were talking about?"

"That's our next job." Tom pointed to a bale of metal foil which he had brought along with the machine parts. "We'll go outside the station and erect this foil in the shape of a huge parabolic reflector. I'll use it to concentrate the sun's rays into a bank of energy-conversion cells just like the ones on the *Challenger*."

After recruiting the help of Ted Spring and several crewmen, Tom explained the job and ordered his work party to don their space suits.

Chow Winkler, who was itching for an excuse to join them, slipped into his galley and returned with a coil of rope. "Boss, I ain't practiced ropin' since I left Texas. You reckon mebbe I could go outside an' try throwin' a few loops while you hombres are workin'?"

Tom grinned at the roly-poly cook. "Sure, pardner. Hop into your space duds!"

One by one, the work party emerged through the station air lock. In spite of the brilliant sunshine which made every object glitter, the space void was an inky black. It was broken only by the steely twinkle of the distant stars and planets.

Two of the crewmen used jet scooters to haul the heavy bale of foil and other equipment. The other members of the work party propelled themselves around by means of the reaction pistols on their suits.

Chow acted especially frisky. "Brand my cosmic sagebrush, I sure wish I had a bronc to ride up here on this sky range!" he proclaimed over his suit radio. "Then I'd really show you buckaroos some fancy ridin'!"

"Maybe I can oblige," Bud signaled back. "I'll tell you where to find a horse in space!"

"You funnin' me again?" Chow demanded.

"No—on the level, Chow," Bud replied.

"Where kin I find this hoss?"

"A mere nine hundred trillion miles away." Bud chuckled. "He's Pegasus, the Winged Horse constellation."

As Chow glared at the youth through his transparent bubble helmet, Tom explained with a grin, "Bud's talking about a group of stars."

"He'll be *seein'* stars one o' these days if he don't stop pullin' my leg!" the cook snorted.

Under Tom's supervision, the bale of metal foil was unfolded and formed into a dish-shaped reflector by means of a wire framework. This in turn was connected to a small motor which would rotate the foil so that it faced the sun at all times.

"Keep it aimed away until we have everything set up for the test," Tom warned his men.

Next he turned his attention to the job of hooking up the energy-conversion cells. These were installed in position near the hub of the space wheel, with conductors leading inside to a transformer in Tom's laboratory.

As work progressed, Chow happily twirled his lariat and practiced tossing a loop around a knob on the station's hull. At first he found it difficult to control his toss while encumbered by his bulky space suit. The lack of gravity also made him misjudge his first throws. But soon the old cowpoke was lassoing the target with expert skill.

"Nice going, old-timer!" Bud applauded. "How about giving me a try?"

"Why sure, Buddy boy," said Chow. He chuckled with satisfaction at this chance to get back at the young copilot. Red-faced, Bud failed again and again to rope the knob.

"I reckon that's not bad for a tenderfoot," Chow sympathized. "You jest keep right on practicin' an' mebbe one o' these days you'll get within a dozen yards or so o' that knob!"

Ted and the other crewmen roared with laughter at Bud's discomfiture. Soon they too were begging for a chance to toss the lariat.

Meanwhile, Tom had gone inside the station to complete the hookup. Bert Everett, one of the crewmen, continued working on the energy-conversion cells.

Suddenly Bud and the others were startled as a piercing scream came over their transiphones.

"Look! It's Bert!" yelled Ted Spring.

To their horror, the men saw Bert's space-suited figure writhing in agony! His limbs thrashed wildly, but he seemed unable to move from the spot where he had been working.

Bud did not waste a second in puzzling out the situation. He triggered his jet pistol and darted to aid the helpless crewman. But as he approached the working area, Bud felt a wave of searing heat pass through his space suit.

In a flash Bud realized what was causing it! Somehow, the foil reflector had been turned toward the sun. Like a burning glass, it was concentrating the sun's rays directly on the spot where Bert Everett was trapped! Not only Bert, but anyone who tried to rescue him, would literally be broiled alive!

"Chow! Get Bert out of here with your lariat!" Bud screamed into his suit mike as he veered away from the danger zone.

Chow responded with the cool skill of a cowboy at roundup time. Grabbing the rope from Ted, he coiled it in a twinkling, and swung the loop above his head. A second later the lariat snaked out through the void and settled around Bert's shoulders. With a yank, Chow dragged the victim to safety!

Cheers rose from the watching crewmen. But they died away in shocked silence after a glimpse at Bert's deathly pale features.

Both Bert and Bud were hustled into the station infirmary. Here their space suits were stripped off, so that the doctor in charge could treat the scorched victims. Fortunately, Bud was unscathed. Bert Everett had suffered a severe shock from the intense rise in temperature inside his space suit. Only the Tomasite covering kept him from instant death. He was put to bed immediately.

"What happened?" Ted asked, as he and the other crewmen stood by his side, still stunned by their comrade's accident.

Tom picked up Bert's discarded space suit and pointed to the jet-pistol attachment in back. "The heat from the reflector fused the jet nozzle so he couldn't fire it," Tom explained. "Without his reaction pistol, he had no way of moving!"

Bert grinned up at them wanly from his hospital bed. "It was like one of those nightmares

*Cheers rose from the watching crewm
as Chow lassoed Bert and pulled him to safe*

where you find yourself rooted to the spot," he commented.

"How do you feel?" Tom asked sympathetically.

"A bit dehydrated, but otherwise okay. By the way, Chow"—Bert turned to the elderly Westerner—"thanks for hauling me out. If you hadn't lassooed me, my goose would have been cooked. I mean *really* cooked!"

"Aw, shucks, 'twarn't nothin'," Chow muttered modestly.

"Oh yes, it was, old-timer," said Tom, putting his arm around Chow's shoulders. "You deserve a medal. And, Bert, if it's any consolation, you've done me quite a service."

"How's that, skipper?" asked Bert.

"Somehow that reflector motor got just enough flow of current to turn it toward the sun. To make sure that doesn't happen again when some-

one's working on the setup, I plan to install a thermostatic alarm system."

At this point, Bud, who had slipped away a few moments before, walked into the compartment. He was carrying a small wrapped package. "For you, Chow," he announced, handing it to the chef. "A small token of my esteem."

Grinning proudly, Chow unwrapped the package. The next moment his grin turned to open-mouthed amazement. Inside lay a small green Texas lizard! Its beady eyes stared up at the old cowpoke as its throat pouch slowly pulsed in and out.

"Great balls o' fire!" For a moment Chow could scarcely believe his eyes, then he turned to Tom. "Brand my prairie cactus, boss, did you *make* this here critter with that machine o' yours?"

CHAPTER XI

A STARTLING DISAPPEARANCE

"NOT guilty, pardner!" Tom grinned.

Chow was baffled. "Well, brand my wild turkey soup, where did this come from?" he muttered, stroking the lizard with his finger. "Poor li'l varmint—I've never seen one so far from home before!"

"Confidentially, it arrived by flying saucer," Bud said with a straight face. As Chow glowered at him suspiciously, Bud exploded with laughter. "Okay, okay. Don't get mad, old-timer. I just borrowed it from the zoology lab!"

Chow was too good-natured to take offense at the joke. Besides, he was touched by the sight of the little reptile from his home range. "Jest for that, I'm a-keepin' this critter for a mascot," he declared. "I'll call him Li'l Ole Alamo."

Tom smiled, patting Chow on the back. "You've earned a reward. And now, how about some grub, pardner?"

The stout old Texan beamed. "Comin' right up, boss!"

After a quick lunch of frankfurters and baked beans, Tom prepared to give his second matter-making machine a tryout. The foil reflector was turned to face the sun. As the energy-conversion cells began to produce electricity, Tom fed power to the machine. The laboratory hummed with the tremendous flow of current.

"How's she perking?" asked Bud after several minutes had gone by.

Tom's face wore a pleased grin. "Really pouring out oxygen!" he replied. "Good thing I arranged to pipe it into the station supply tanks, or we'd be space-happy on the stuff!"

"Are you going to try to make solid matter?" asked Ted.

Tom nodded as he studied the wave pattern on the scope and adjusted several tuning knobs. Then he pushed one of the element control buttons. "We'll try carbon first," he explained. "That's a basic element in all organic compounds."

The young inventor stood by tensely as the space solartron throbbed into action. He watched the control dials like a hawk, making frequent adjustments as the needles flickered back and forth.

Minutes crept by . . . half an hour . . . then an hour. Finally Tom checked the receiving tank. It contained a thinly sprinkled deposit of a black powdery substance!

"Magic!" Bud exclaimed. "Don't keep us in suspense, Tom. *Is* it carbon?"

Tom rubbed some between his thumb and forefinger. "Looks like carbon, all right," Tom replied, his heart pounding. "But I'll check to make sure." He tested the substance with his Swift spectroscope, then nodded without speaking.

"You don't look exactly overjoyed," Ted remarked. "This rates a cheer, doesn't it?"

Tom grinned wryly. "The machine works, if that's what you mean. But at this rate of production, it wouldn't do us much good on the moon or on a space cruise."

"How come?" asked Bud. "Too slow?"

"Way too slow," Tom said. "It's the same old problem—not enough power. Which means our real test run will have to wait until Arv gets those energy collectors finished."

Tom concluded his experiments by trying to make two more elements needed in food or fuel compounds—hydrogen and nitrogen. Since hydrogen gas is highly combustible, Tom throttled down the machine so as to produce only a small amount. However, the results showed clearly that the solartron could generate either kind of gas in large quantities.

"My congratulations, son!" said Mr. Swift, after hearing Tom's report. "On the basis of this first test, I feel certain that your machine's performance will be up to all expectations when the energy collectors are ready. Meanwhile, perhaps you fellows would like to help on my cosmic dust project?"

Tom, Bud, and Ted were eager to do so. Acting on Mr. Swift's instructions, they rigged a powerful set of electrodes on the hub of the space wheel. The elder scientist busied himself setting up a special wave-generating apparatus inside the station.

When the setup was complete, Mr. Swift closed a switch, beaming out an ultrahigh-frequency ionization ray. The boys checked the electrodes every few minutes. Bit by bit, the cosmic dust particles began to build up around the positive electrode. By the time Chow sounded the dinner gong, the particles had formed a stone, possessing a metallic luster and looking somewhat like a small meteorite.

"Not bad for a first try." Mr. Swift smiled as he examined the results. "But I seem to be up against the same problem you are, Tom—my process works rather slowly."

"The particles may accumulate faster as the attracting surface increases in size, Dad," Tom pointed out. "Let's continue the experiment tomorrow. I'm eager to see how this works out."

The next morning, however, while the station crew was eating breakfast, Arv Hanson arrived by shuttle rocket from Fearing Island.

"The luxium and conductate leaves are finished, Tom," he reported. "So are the frameworks of foil tubing. I made up enough for a dozen energy collectors."

"Good work, Arv!" Tom approved. "Let's get them unloaded and we'll assemble one in my lab."

With Arv and Bud assisting—Ted would remain with Mr. Swift—Tom set to work immediately. Each set of luxium-conductate leaves was installed in the crisscross framework of tubing and folded over until there was a great pile. Then the wiring was connected. Hours went by. It was midafternoon before the job was finished.

"Whew!" gasped Bud wearily. "That was like working a four-acre crossword puzzle!"

"This is only the beginning, fly boy." Tom grinned. "We still have to test twelve more."

Finally, with more assistance, the work was accomplished. Each of the huge energy collectors was neatly folded and baled into a compact bundle and transferred to the spaceship one by one.

"Are you still going to use helium gas for inflating the tubes?" asked Arv.

"Yes," Tom replied. "But first I'd like to get Dad's advice on the proper inflation pressure."

The young inventor hurried into his father's laboratory, only to find it empty. A crewman told him that Mr. Swift and Ted Spring had gone outside the station to work on the cosmic dust experiment.

Tom donned his space suit and went out through the air lock. To his amazement, neither Ted nor Mr. Swift was in sight around the space wheel. When Tom came back inside, thinking the crewman had been mistaken, he used the loud-speaker system, but still he could not locate his father and Ted in any of the station compartments.

Worried, Tom said to Ken Horton, "Where *are* they?"

"I know they went outside," Ken insisted. "They both checked with me personally, but they never checked in. And your dad laid down that rule himself for keeping tabs on every person at the outpost."

"They're not there now," Tom replied tersely.

Fearing that the two might have drifted off into the void, Tom ordered the station telescope brought into play. But a complete sweep of the surrounding area revealed no trace of the missing pair.

Meanwhile, the radio and radar operators were busy at their sets. They too failed to make contact. Repeated call signals brought no response, and the radarscopes showed no object within range which might be a space-suited human.

By this time Tom was frantic with worry. Bud tried to console him, saying Mr. Swift surely would not have done anything foolish, but Tom could not be comforted.

"They're gone," he insisted. "Probably lost." Tom gripped a nearby bulkhead nervously. "Shall I notify Mother and Sandy? And how about Mrs. Spring? She's apt to go to pieces if she thinks anything has happened to Ted!"

Chow Winkler had come out of the galley as soon as he heard the news. The stout cook laid a hand on Tom's arm as the young inventor paced back and forth. "Now look here, boss," Chow said sympathetically, "wearin' a hole in the deck ain't gonna help none. How 'bout callin' Harlan Ames? Mebbe he can give you some kind o' lead."

"Good idea, Chow," Tom agreed.

Within a few moments he had contacted Ames at Enterprises and explained the situation. "Have you heard from Dad?" he asked.

"No, Tom. This *is* serious. Haven't you any idea what happened to Mr. Swift and Ted?"

"Just one theory," the young inventor replied. "They may have gone a distance from the outpost and been caught in some freakish magnetic stream and couldn't use their radios. No telling how far it might have carried them. Well, since you haven't heard from Dad, I'm going out in the *Challenger* and find him!"

"I'm glad to hear that," said Ames. "And for the time being, I think you'd better keep the disappearance of your father and Ted a secret. No point in frightening your mother or Mrs. Spring unnecessarily."

"I'll do that, Harlan," Tom promised. "And I'll keep you posted. Roger."

The *Challenger* was quickly prepared for take-off. Besides Tom, Bud, and the regular crew, both Arv Hanson and Chow Winkler volunteered to go along.

"Never flew a search pattern in space before," Bud remarked as Tom sent the mighty ship zooming away from the outpost. "How do we do it?"

"By computer," Tom replied. "I've already fed in the data about the time of disappearance and the maximum possible speed they could make of their own volition. From here on, the ship will be guided by electronic brain in the most efficient search pattern."

Half an hour later, the radarman reported to Tom from the communications room, "Something on the screen, skipper! A fast-moving object, elevation twelve degrees, port forward quadrant. Can't make it out!"

Tom swiveled the repelatrons and swung the ship upward in a speedy turn. A streak of pips flashed across their radar screen.

"Only an extra large meteor!" Tom groaned, after chasing it for several moments.

Three hours went by as they circled the space station in wide-ranging sweeps. But in spite of constant vigilance, they picked up no clues to the fate of Mr. Swift and Ted.

Weary and discouraged, but unwilling to admit defeat, Tom steered for the phantom satellite, Nestria. This tiny asteroid had been moved into orbit around the earth by some unknown creatures in outer space, with whom the Swifts had established friendly communication. The space beings had intended this as a first step toward visiting earth, but so far had been unable to master all the problems involved.

"Gonna take a look-see on Little Luna, boss?"

Chow asked as the rocky moonlet loomed into view.

Tom nodded grimly. "It's a faint hope, Chow, but we have nothing to lose."

Months before, Tom had led a space expedition to explore the satellite. He had christened it Nestria in honor of his mother, Mary Nestor Swift, but Bud's original nickname of "Little Luna" still clung.

Soon the asteroid filled their view panes. Rugged and barren, except for the installations planted by Tom's group, the moonlet's surface was shadowed by yellow craters and upthrusting crags of pink, gray, and blue.

Tom cruised around the satellite, remembering most of the terrain from his previous visit. Neither radar nor telescope, however, detected any sign of a recent landing.

"What do you think, skipper?" asked Arv, breaking the silence.

"Hopeless. I'm afraid," Tom replied in a dejected voice.

Suddenly Bud snapped his fingers. "Hey! Why not call your space friends, Tom? They seem to know almost everything that goes on. In fact, maybe they had something to do with your dad's disappearance!"

Tom brightened at the suggestion. "Smart thinking, Bud. It's worth a try."

Some months before, the Swifts had received their first message from the space people. It had been etched on a black meteorlike missile which had plunged to earth at Enterprises. Tom and his father had been successful in translating the queer mathematical symbols on the missile. Later, they had "talked" to the senders in code, using a powerful transmitter. Incoming signals were picked up on a new type of oscilloscope which Tom had invented.

Arv now took over the ship's controls while the two boys hurried down to the radio compartment. Tom beamed out a message, explaining the situation and asking for information about Mr. Swift and Ted.

Minutes went by. Both boys watched the scope intently. But no symbols flashed on the screen.

Tom's heart sank. "Bud," the young inventor said grimly, "it begins to look as if Dad and Ted have been kidnaped!"

CHAPTER XII

MESSAGE FROM NOWHERE

"KIDNAPED!" Bud exclaimed. "You mean by your space friends?"

Tom shrugged. "Perhaps. But more probably by some earth enemies of ours. Don't forget, there are plenty of troublemakers like Hampshire. Also, spies and criminals who would do almost anything to learn the secrets of Dad's and my inventions."

Bud chilled as he realized the truth of Tom's words. More than once, not only back home in Shopton, but under the ocean and in wild corners of the globe, the young inventor had had to battle ruthless enemies who sought to steal the fruits of the Swifts' scientific genius.

"Buck up, pal," Bud said stoutly. "We'll find 'em—and soon!"

Nevertheless, it was a gloomy crew of searchers who returned to the space station aboard the *Challenger*.

"Any luck?" asked Ken Horton as the station

crew gathered around anxiously to hear the news.

Tom shook his head. "Looks as if we have three choices—a natural phenomenon, the space people, and earth enemies. If it's the last group, we'll probably hear from them."

The young inventor was too downhearted to blame the radarmen who should have detected any marauders on their scopes. But Chow reeled off a few scorching remarks of his own.

"I ain't namin' no names," the cook growled, "but if certain hombres had been keepin' watch like they were supposed to, no kidnapers could 'a' gotten within a hundred miles o' this here spread!"

"Now, wait a minute, Chow!" A tall, lanky radarman stepped forward angrily. "I was manning the detection radar from twelve to four, and I can guarantee I didn't miss any blips on the scope!"

Tom's eyes sparked with interest. "In that case," he declared, "our enemy must have a powerful device that drew Dad and Ted off to a great distance and *then* took them into a spaceship!"

Bud clenched his hands. "Just like that animal rocket was drawn off so mysteriously during our race to the moon. I'll bet this proves your space friends are the ones your dad is with!"

Because a strange disease was attacking the animal life on their planet, the space people had recently sent a rocket containing infected animals, hoping the Swifts might find a cure. Later, after the infection was conquered, the ship was propelled away by some mysterious and invisible force.

"You may be right at that, Bud." Tom frowned thoughtfully.

"Sure, I'm right," said Bud cheerfully. "And I wouldn't call them kidnapers either. Remember, your dad had a radio in his space suit, so he could have called for help. I have a hunch that when a chance came to go off with the space people, he just couldn't resist the temptation. You'll hear from him, skipper, and probably soon."

"I sure hope so," Tom said.

He was not altogether convinced and took the *Challenger* out on trip after trip, hoping to find a clue to the missing pair. He was in constant touch with Harlan Ames. But two days went by without any report from Mr. Swift or Ted. Tom's fears mounted. Even if his father had had no chance to signal by radio at the time he left, Tom thought, surely he would have sent news by now, if he were with friendly beings.

On the third day after the disappearance, Tom was trying to eat some breakfast, although he had no appetite, when a radioman came rushing into the mess compartment.

"Hey, skipper!" he shouted, waving a sheet of paper. "We've just had word on your father!"

Tom sprang from the bench, amid a babble of excitement. "Word from where, Steve? What's the news?"

"I don't know who sent the message," the radio-man replied. "The sender didn't identify him-self. Here, read this!" He thrust the paper into Tom's hand.

Tom read the message aloud to the eager crewmen:

TOM SWIFT, OUTPOST IN SPACE. YOUR FATHER AND COMPANION ARE SAFE. FUR-THER INFORMATION WILL FOLLOW.

"See! I told you, pal!" Bud exclaimed. "Your dad and Ted *must* be with the space people!"

"I'm not so sure, Bud," the young inventor replied slowly. "They've never communicated with us before in our own language."

"They've never had your dad aboard their spaceship before," Bud pointed out. "He prob-ably worded the message for them."

"Could be," Tom muttered. "If so, let's hope he signs the next one in person before I go off my rocker wondering what's happened!"

To keep his mind off his worries, Tom plunged back to work on his solartron. He made several more experiments in his laboratory and then asked Arv and Bud to help him install the ma-chine in the *Challenger*.

"We'll try it out with the energy collectors," Tom told them. "If the setup works okay, we can start planning for a moon expedition."

"Lead on, Moon Boy!" Bud whooped.

Within two hours, the matter maker had been torn down and reassembled on board the spaceship. The energy collectors, baled into small bundles, were there already, leaving only the tanks of helium gas to be stacked on the ship.

Soon the *Challenger* was streaking off from the outpost. Tom continued to increase the speed, then settled into an orbit far from the station.

"Where do we stage the test, skipper?" Arv Hanson asked.

"This area will do," Tom replied, easing off on the repelatrons.

With the ship coasting along at orbital speed, Arv, Tom, and two of the crewmen donned space suits and hauled the energy collectors out through the air lock. Standing on the ship's landing platform, they unloosened the bales, then nudged them off into the void, using jet scooters. The free ends of the gas tubing were fed back into the ship through a special airtight fitting on the hull.

"All set, skipper?" Bud's voice came over the intercom after the work party had returned to the ship. Tom and Arv had gone to the compartment where the solartron and gas tanks had been installed.

"All set," Tom replied. "Watch through the view panes and tell me how the sheets unfold."

"Roger!"

Opening the stopcocks on the gas tanks, Tom fed helium into the tubing.

"Going fine, Tom!" was Bud's report. "The

sheets are opening without a hitch!" A few moments later he added, "Okay. Shut off the gas! They're wide open now!"

Tense with excitement, Tom and Arv hurried up to the flight compartment where Bud was tending the controls. A thrilling spectacle greeted their eyes through the pilots' windows. Streaming off in the blackness of the void, the energy collectors had opened to their full extent, like vast silver lace sails. The tubes glistened with dazzling brilliance in the sunshine. The sheets reflected no light.

"Man, what a sight!" cheered one of the crew who had gathered to watch the experiment.

"Space-age windjammer, that's us!" Bud quipped.

"They really are like sails," Tom remarked. "Only instead of using wind, they'll be drawing power from the—"

His words ended in a gasp as one of the collectors suddenly billowed out of shape and began fluttering wildly in the void.

"Skipper, what's wrong?" cried out Arv, clutching Tom by the arm.

"I don't know, but I'd better find out pronto!"

Donning his space suit hastily, Tom rushed out through the air lock and propelled himself off the landing platform with his jet pistol. The others watched through the view panes.

They saw the young inventor streak toward the billowing energy collector. He reached it and began skimming along its surface, evidently trying to find out what was causing the trouble. Suddenly the framework of foil tubing began to rip loose from the cell leaves!

"Good night! The whole thing's coming apart!" Bud cried out.

Like waving tentacles, the tubes and wiring began to envelop Tom. He was trapped like a fish in a net! His comrades saw him struggle desperately to free himself from the tangle.

"Brand my octopus stew, he's all roped an' hogtied!" Chow babbled. "Quick! Someone get me my space suit! I'm goin' out there an' save him!"

"And I'm going with you!" Bud added. "Take over the controls, Arv!"

The copilot scrambled down to the hangar deck, and Chow was close behind him. But by the time they had climbed into their space suits and emerged through the air lock, they saw Tom returning safely to the ship.

"What happened?" Bud called anxiously over his suit radio.

"Loose joint somewhere in the tubing," Tom reported. "The gas leaked out under pressure, and eventually the whole sheet went blooey."

"You all right, boss?" Chow asked.

"Sure thing." Tom grinned. "It was a tough fight, but I finally got myself untangled. How about you two helping me reel up some of that loose tubing?"

"You came to the right party, son," Chow boasted. "Reckon that won't be no job at all for an ole lariat expert like me!"

After twenty minutes of work, the three managed to salvage most of the foil tubing and cell leaves. Then they returned to the *Challenger*.

"I'll start experiments with the solartron, using the other collectors," Tom announced.

To everyone's delight, the machine worked to perfection, producing simple elements in large quantities. Tom, instead of being thrilled over the outcome, seemed halfhearted and listless.

"Guess he's worried sick about his dad," Arv Hanson whispered to Chow.

The old cowpoke bustled down to his galley. "Reckon I can cheer him up with a nice tasty mess o' vittles," he told himself.

Cooking was a matter of minutes on the ship's electronic range. A short time later Chow rode up in the elevator to the flight deck with a loaded dinner tray. From the covered dishes wafted the delicious aroma of corn fritters, T-Bone steak, and hot mince pie.

"Good night, Chow! What's all this?" Tom exclaimed as the cook came into the pilot's cabin. "Up here in space one can't tell whether it's time for breakfast, lunch, or dinner, but this looks like all three of today's meals rolled into one."

"I'll tell you what it is," said Chow. "A special feast for the smartest young inventor on earth or in space!" He lifted the dish covers, one by one, and displayed his culinary triumphs.

Tom smiled and thanked Chow gratefully. He tried to eat with a show of appetite while the cook stood beaming over him. But after the Westerner left the compartment, the young inventor barely picked at the food. All his fears and worries over the fate of his father and Ted Spring seemed to come crowding back on him.

"Am I doing the right thing not telling Mother?" Tom fretted. Yet he dreaded the thought of breaking the news to her. "I'll talk it over with Ames again," he decided.

Shoving his tray aside with the food less than half eaten, Tom hurried down to the radio compartment. In a few moments he made contact with Harlan Ames at Enterprises.

"Hi, Tom! I was just going to call you," the security chief said. "I have some news."

CHAPTER XIII

THE SECRET FORMULA

"NEWS about Dad?" Tom asked eagerly.

"Not directly," Ames replied, "but it may have some connection with your father's disappearance."

"Let's hear it!"

Ames's news concerned the *Enterprises Journal.* When the first issue was sent out to a restricted mailing list, one of the scientists who received a copy had phoned in a surprising bit of information. He pointed out that a certain formula which appeared in one of the articles had nothing to do with the subject matter of that particular article.

"I checked back on the formula," Ames continued, "and it turned out to be part of the circuit design for your new solartron." He read off the formula.

"Good grief, Harlan!" Tom exclaimed. "That was supposed to be top-secret! I'm sure it wasn't

114

in the article when Dad and I went over the papers!"

"You're right," Ames said. "It wasn't. We got hold of the original typewritten manuscripts from the printer and found that someone had inserted the formula in pencil."

"Who was the 'someone'?" Tom asked.

"We haven't been able to find out yet," the security chief said, "but I have a hunch it was an inside job."

"An inside job!" Tom was shocked. Then he remembered again the eavesdropper who had knocked over the chemical equipment in his office, and also the suspected sabotage of the printing plates. Perhaps the same person was responsible for all three incidents. "Any clues, Harlan?"

"Not so far. But we learned that Miss Warner left the papers on her desk while she went out to lunch. In fact she didn't take the papers to the printer until late afternoon. That would have given the culprit plenty of opportunity to write in the formula."

"But why? What's the angle?" Tom puzzled.

"Only one reason that I can figure out," Ames replied. "Remember, that formula was long and complicated, with a bunch of mathematical signs and Greek letters in it."

"So?"

"So it was probably too tough to memorize," Ames went on. "And it was too risky to carry it out of the plant written down on paper, since every employee is checked at the gate. But this way he could get the formula outside Enterprises without any danger of being caught."

"Hmm, that could be the answer," Tom mused.

The young inventor was deeply disturbed. He knew that the *Journal* had been mailed to a large group of scientists. Undoubtedly one of them was a subversive, with an accomplice in Swift Enterprises.

"Keep working on it, Harlan," Tom said, "and make sure none of the rest of the formula for the solartron leaks out. In the meantime, do you think we should tell mother and Mrs. Spring about Dad and Ted's disappearance?"

Ames mulled over the problem. "Still no leads?" he asked.

Tom reported the unsigned radio message, but added that he was not sure it had come from the space people.

"In that case, skipper," said Ames, "I think we should tell your mother and Sandy. Suppose we let your mother decide whether or not to inform Mrs. Spring and Ray?"

Tom agreed to this plan, and Ames promised to break the news as gently as possible the following morning. "It's late here. I'm sure she's in bed now."

Before starting back for the outpost, Tom ordered the power gatherers deflated, folded, and put back into the ship for future use. Then, while most of the men slept, he set the *Challenger's* course.

When the great spaceship reached the outpost,

Ken Horton greeted Tom with a look of excitement as he entered through the station air lock.

"We've just picked up a faint SOS, skipper," Ken reported. "It came from space."

Tom's pulse raced with sudden hope. "You think it was from Dad and Ted?" he asked tensely.

"I don't know. The radioman said the message trailed off before he could catch all of it. But it sounded like just one man, because the wording was 'I am stranded in orbit—' not 'we are stranded.'"

"How about his position? Did you get a fix?"

"Approximately," Ken replied. "He was about 12,000 miles above the Pacific, somewhere around 20 degrees north latitude and 130 degrees west longitude. Orbiting on a northeasterly track."

After inquiring the time of the call, Tom gave orders to his crew to re-embark immediately aboard the *Challenger* for a rescue operation. All data on the stranded spaceman was fed into a computer which supplied the proper course and speed to the ship's navigating instruments. In a few moments the great silver space craft was spearing downward to intercept the derelict.

"Got it, skipper!" the radarman called over the intercom. "Twelve degrees starboard, elevation minus five!"

"There he is!" Bud cried a moment later, pointing through his copilot's window.

A small rocket ship was drifting in the inky void with its final stage still clinging, half-locked, to the nose section.

Tom flicked on the radio and spoke into his microphone. "Swift ship *Challenger* calling stranded rocket! Can you read me?"

"Rocket to *Challenger*," came the reply. "I can read you and see you. My third stage is jammed and I'm marooned in orbit. Can you take me aboard?"

"Roger. Who are you?"

"My name is Selwyn Joss," the space voyager replied. "I blasted off this morning from one of the Marshall Islands. Destination moon—but this is as far as I got."

"You took off by yourself?" Tom asked unbelievingly.

"Sure. Why not? It's a one-man ship."

Tom and Bud exchanged startled glances. Bud pointed one finger to his head and twirled the finger as if to say, "The guy must be crazy!"

Tom grinned and spoke into his mike again. "Okay, Joss. Stand by for rescue. We'll come into orbit just ahead of you and take your ship in tow."

Switching to manual control, Tom guided the *Challenger* skillfully into position ahead of the space derelict. A few moments later the *Challenger's* air lock opened. Tom, Bud, and a pair of crewmen emerged, bearing coils of light, tough nylon cable.

"Secure one end of each cable to our repelatron rails," Tom ordered over his suit radio. "Hook on the other end any place you can find a projection on the rocket. We may have to run the lines all the way aft to his motor compartment."

As the crewmen performed their task, another space-suited figure appeared. It was Joss, the rocket pilot, crawling out of his tiny flight compartment.

"Can I give you any help?" he radioed. "I— I've never been out in the void before. . . . Whew!"

Tom looked up sharply and saw the spaceman waver crazily, then clutch at the ship's air lock.

"Help him, Bud!" Tom cried. "He's space-happy!"

Bud darted to the pilot's aid. Evidently Joss had succumbed to the awful giddiness of space and its bleak sense of emptiness. Bud helped him find a handhold on one of the cables, then guided him gently toward the hatch of the *Challenger.*

In a few minutes Tom and his crewmen finished connecting the towline and returned to their own ship.

"How is he?" asked Tom, re-entering the flight compartment.

"I'm okay now," Joss spoke up with a wan smile. Bud and Chow had helped him out of his space suit. "Had a slight touch of space sickness, I guess. This is my first trip out."

"So I gathered," said Tom dryly. Inwardly he was wondering if the man might be putting on an act. Could it be that Joss was a spy, connected with the kidnapers responsible for his Dad's and

Ted's disappearance? "Mind telling us how you expected to land on the moon and get back to earth safely all by yourself?"

"Maybe it was foolhardy," Joss admitted, "but I saw no reason to risk someone else's life."

The rescued rocketeer was in his thirties, stockily built, and had thinning reddish hair. He explained that his father, a fabulously wealthy man, was owner of the Joss Manufacturing Company. He and his son had hoped to gain publicity by the moon-rocket stunt.

"Mighty expensive publicity if it had cost you your life," Bud observed.

"I guess you're right," Joss said ruefully. "But when I started out, I really thought I could make it."

Tom questioned him further, and finally decided that Joss had had nothing to do with the disappearance of his father and Ted Spring. Moreover, he had not seen them or picked up any messages.

"We'll take you to our space station and send you back to earth safely," Tom promised. "Sorry we can't offer you much hospitality, but our installation up here is top-secret. Government orders, you understand."

"Sure, sure, I realize that," Joss replied. "Believe me, I'm grateful to you for saving my life. I'd have gotten mighty tired of orbiting around here for the next umpteen million years!"

Tom knew from the shuttle-rocket schedule that a ship was due from Fearing Island within the next two hours. It arrived soon after their return to the outpost. Selwyn Joss was escorted aboard and his craft stored in the cargo compartment.

"So long and thanks again!" Joss called back over the radio.

"Have a good trip," Tom replied.

As soon as the ship had blasted off, he contacted George Dilling at Fearing Island over the company's special frequency. Tom gave orders for Joss to be transported to the mainland as soon as he landed. "I think the man's okay," he added, "but have Harlan Ames make a follow-up check on him, just to play safe."

"Wilco!" Dilling replied.

Tom had hardly signed off when another voice crackled over the radio. "Tom, come and get us! We're on the moon!"

It was Ted Spring's voice!

CHAPTER XIV

MOON SEARCH

TOM and his companions were electrified! Mr. Swift and Ted Spring were on the moon!

Everyone listened intently as the message continued. "We were drawn away from the space station by some kind of invisible force ray," Ted went on. "I'm not sure what happened after that. Tom, your dad and I both blacked out."

Mr. Swift's voice broke in, "The important thing is that the two of us are here on the moon. Come and get us and hurry!"

Abruptly the voices ceased.

Tom grabbed the microphone. "Dad! Ted! Can you hear me?" he called urgently. "This is Tom at the outpost! Come in, please!"

There was no response. Finally Tom gave up trying to contact them.

"Come on!" he told the others. "We'll take off right now! We must rescue them!"

"I'm with you, pal!" Bud shouted.

Arv Hanson, however, clutched Tom's arm.

122

"Wait a while, skipper," he begged. "That call may be a trick. If your dad and Ted were captured by some enemy, they wouldn't be released without some good reason."

"What do you mean?" Tom asked impatiently.

"If we go zooming off to the moon now, we may be heading right into a trap!"

Chow looked worried. "Brand my biscuits, Arv may be right, boss," the cook opined. "Them space rustlers didn't plan that kidnapin' just for a joke. Mebbe they're fixin' to bushwhack us!"

"But what about Dad's and Ted's oxygen supply?" Tom protested. "If they *are* stranded up there, it may give out!"

Arv's face was flushed and uneasy. "I know how you must feel, Tom, but let's find out what Horton thinks. Check with Harlan Ames too."

When Ken Horton was informed of the radio message, he suggested that Tom wait until Mr. Swift and Ted made contact again. Ames, too, when reached at Enterprises, agreed with this advice.

"That call sounds fishy to me, Tom," he said. "Why did they stop so abruptly and not respond to *your* signal? And another thing, would their suit radios have range enough to transmit their voices from the moon?"

"I'm not sure, Harlan," Tom pondered. "It would depend on various conditions, but you may have a point there. Guess we'd better wait."

Harassed by fears and doubts, the young inventor found it hard to hold his impatience in check. To be prepared for any emergency, Tom ordered the *Challenger* stocked at once with all supplies and equipment needed for a moon expedition.

"How about giving your space solartron another workout?" Bud suggested, to keep his friend's mind occupied. "You still haven't tried combining any of those elements you concocted and making some food."

The idea intrigued Tom enough to try it. "I'll start with some simple compounds," he said.

After boarding the *Challenger*, the two boys, Chow, and Doc Simpson unloaded the power gatherers and put them in place on the outside of the ship. The helium was sent into the tubing, then the watchers crowded into the compartment where the solartron was set up. They watched in fascination as Tom switched on the current and adjusted the controls.

"What'll it be first, skipper?" Doc asked.

"Let's try making sugar," Tom decided. "All it takes is carbon, hydrogen, and oxygen."

He pushed several buttons on the element and isotope control panels, then watched the wave pattern closely on the oscilloscope. Minutes later, he stopped the machine. Over a pound of sugar had crystallized in the receiving tank!

"Wal, I'll be a locoed bronc!" Chow gasped. He scooped up some of the glistening white grains unbelievingly. "You sure this stuff is sugar, son?"

Tom tested some with a Swift spectroscope, then nodded, grinning. "Taste it."

Chow did so, somewhat gingerly. His sun-bronzed leathery face cracked into a broad smile. "Boss, this takes the cake!" he exclaimed. "Machine-made groceries! Brand my coyote cutlets, I never would 'a' believed it!"

"Chow," said Tom, "get me some spoons, dishes, a bowl, and an egg beater from the galley, will you?"

As the cook hurried off, Tom resumed his production of simple food compounds. He made citric acid, several fats resembling corn oil, a gelatinlike protein substance, and finally water. When Chow returned with the utensils, Tom mixed the gelatin in water, added some sugar and citric acid, and set the mixture aside to jell. Finally he whipped the fats, water, and the remaining sugar into a texture similar to whipped cream.

"To top off our lemon gelatin," Tom explained. The others were speechless.

After it had jelled, Tom served a dishful to each man. In a moment they were smacking their lips and pronouncing the concoction delicious.

"It's nourishing too," said Doc Simpson. "A person could live on it indefinitely."

"Of course, sirloin steak and onions might taste good for a change, every so often," Bud remarked.

"Give me time." Tom grinned. "With a little experimenting, I might come up with something that tastes like steer."

"Reckon the Texas cattle business is safe for a while yet," Chow remarked. "But this stuff sure tastes a heap better'n some o' them dried-up rations we used to take on space cruises!"

"Better watch out, Chow, or this solartron may put *you* out of business," Bud teased.

"A good cook ain't never out of a job, son," Chow retorted calmly.

"You can say that again, Chow!" Tom chuckled, slapping the old Westerner fondly on the back.

After much urging, Tom was persuaded to lie down for a nap. He found himself more tired than he realized and finally dropped off to sleep. But almost at once, it seemed, his radio was flashing him awake. Ken Horton was calling from the space station.

"Tom, we just had another radio call from your dad and Ted!"

"I want to talk to them!" Tom cried, springing up from his bunk.

"Can't do it," Ken answered. "The call was just like last time. Both Mr. Swift and Ted said a few sentences and then signed off. When we tried to signal your dad, he didn't respond, or Ted either."

Tom groaned with frustration. "What did they say?"

"Same thing. They're on the moon and want you to come and get them. One thing, though,"

Ken added, "we got a fix on their signal and it *was* definitely coming from the moon."

"That's good enough for me," Tom declared. "Pass the word to embark. We'll unhook the power gatherers. Same crew as before, plus Doc Simpson."

Everyone responded eagerly. Soon the powerful space craft was zooming moonward. When it was well underway, Tom ordered his crew to rotate watches—each man to snatch an hour's sleep at a time.

Later, when Chow was serving cocoa and sandwiches, the intercom buzzed in the flight compartment. "Just picked up another call from your dad, skipper!" the radioman reported.

"Anything new?" Tom asked tensely.

"He said you'd find him and Ted Spring in the same location where you made your landing on the moon last time. That was all. Then he signed off."

"Okay. Thanks, Marty," Tom said. "Keep monitoring the same frequency."

"Roger!"

Bud flashed the young pilot a questioning glance. "I suppose your dad meant when you and I landed on the repelatron donkeys."

The "donkeys" were small flying platforms, also nicknamed flying carpets, which Tom had invented for moon transport work on his earlier trip. Each platform was about three feet square, with a housing for the repelatron which held it aloft by force ray. The pilot steered by means of a small hand-control box at the end of a six-foot wire.

Bud asked, "Tom, do you think the message from your dad was on the level?"

Tom shrugged uneasily. "I don't know, Bud. I can't figure out why neither Dad nor Ted will respond to our calls. It doesn't make sense."

As Tom gunned the repelatrons to full power, they blazed through the void at cometlike speed. No one broke the tense silence. All eyes in the flight compartment were glued to the view panes.

Ahead of them the moon loomed with a white and ghostly radiance. Its face was pock-marked with craters and ridged with jagged mountain ranges, while the lunar plains or "seas" showed as smooth dark patches.

In two more hours the *Challenger* was hovering a hundred miles above the moon's surface. Tom steered for the Crater of Copernicus, scene of his previous landing.

"Take over the controls, Bud!" he ordered.

Eagerly Tom focused the ship's powerful telescope and scanned the terrain below. Light-colored streaks radiated outward from the rim of the crater. Inside the towering rock walls, the bowl-like surface was strewn with gritty dust and rubble.

"See anything?" Hanson asked.

Tom shook his head. "Not a trace of a recent landing so far as I can make out. Cruise around in widening circles, Bud."

What would they find inside? Tom wondered tensely

The crater was fifty or sixty miles in width and the telescope showed every detail of its interior with needle-sharp clarity. Yet Tom could discern no evidence of movement, nor unusual marks in the gritty debris.

Grim-faced with disappointment, Tom turned the telescope over to Arv Hanson and went back to the controls. He brought the ship still lower and began circling farther and farther beyond the crater. Yawning cracks and crevices, spiny mountain ridges, and tumbled heaps of rocks passed below them.

"Hold it, skipper!" Arv cried. "Go back over that stretch of lava sand we just passed."

Tom swiveled the steering repelatrons to turn the ship around, then retraced his course slowly.

"There it is!" Arv shouted. "Tom, I believe that's a rocket half-buried in the sand!"

Tense with excitement, Tom got up to peer through the telescope, while Bud held the ship hovering over the spot. "You're right, Arv," the young inventor said tersely. "Want to come along while I examine it, Bud?"

"Sure do. Take over, will you, Arv?"

The two boys hurried down to the hangar deck, donned their space suits, and carried two repelatron donkeys out through the air lock. They sailed off the ship's landing platform and swooped downward. What would they find inside? Tom wondered tensely.

As soon as the donkey touched ground, Tom leaped off and ran to examine the rocket more closely. There was no hatch or other opening in the part sticking above the sand.

Eager to find out if the rocket held an occupant, Tom tapped out a message in International Code. He held his ear close to the hull, but could detect no response.

"Bud, we *must* find out if anyone's inside!" the young inventor said urgently. "Help me turn it over!"

CHAPTER XV

THE HALF-BURIED ROCKET

EXCITEDLY the two boys pushed and tugged at the rocket. But it had plowed too deeply into the ground to be loosened easily.

"Now what?" Bud asked.

Lacking digging tools, he and Tom were at a disadvantage.

"Let's kick at the dirt," Tom suggested.

Together the boys clawed at the coarse lava sand with their boots. Finally they freed the rocket and turned it over.

"There's the entry hatch," said Tom, pointing to a closely fitting door outlined in the hull.

"How do we open it?" Bud asked.

"Hmm, good question."

Tom fingered the hatch until he found a place where it yielded to pressure and the door sprang open. Tom and Bud gasped at the contents. There was no one inside. Instead, the rocket contained a mass of electronic equipment, including several tape recorders and a powerful radio transmitter.

"Well, for Pete's sake!" Bud cried out. "What does this mean? Did the rocket land here by mistake?"

"No, it was sent here on purpose. It's tuned to our special frequency." Tom said grimly after a glance at the dial.

"You mean this is what's been sending us those radio messages we thought were from your father and Ted?"

Tom nodded, tight-lipped. "I'd bet on it. Let's check these recording tapes."

"Good night! Don't touch the stuff, Tom!" Bud begged. "It may have some kind of alarm mechanism that will warn your enemy we're here!"

The words were hardly out of his mouth when one of the tape recorders switched on automatically and began to play. Ted Spring's voice came blaring out of the loud-speaker.

"Calling Tom Swift at the outpost! This is Ted Spring speaking. Come and rescue us, Tom! Your father and I are stranded on the moon!"

Mr. Swift's voice joined in. *"Please come at once, son. We can't hold out much longer. Our location on the moon is near the same spot where you landed before."*

Tom and Bud exchanged stunned glances as the broadcast ended. "There's your answer, Bud," the young inventor muttered. "If you ask me, Dad and Ted have never been near this place. The rocket was sent to the moon to lure us up here!"

"Then Arv was right!" Bud exclaimed. "We've walked into a trap!"

Ruefully Tom admitted that this could be true and an attack might be imminent.

"Then let's clear out pronto!" Bud urged. "Why wait for them to capture us?" He started to steer off.

Tom grinned wryly through his transparent bubble helmet. "Relax, pal. If they've already detected us, there's no point in trying to sneak off. Now that we're here, let's find out as much as we can."

"Like for instance?" Bud inquired, still feeling that they should leave at once.

"You go over the rocket and see if you can find any markings which might give us a clue to the sender," Tom replied. "In the meantime, I want to examine these tapes. I have a hunch the pattern is a broadcast every four hours."

The boys conducted their examination as tensely as if they were handling a time bomb.

"No luck," Bud reported a few minutes later. "I've been over every inch of the hull and motor section. She's clean as a whistle."

"Well, *I've* found out something," Tom said. "These tapes have been spliced."

"Spliced?" Bud was puzzled. "You mean—"

"I mean these messages are as phony as a nine-dollar bill! They've been pieced together out of entirely different conversations."

"Oh, now I get it!" Bud exclaimed. "They quizzed your dad and Ted for hours, and recorded every word they said. Then they snipped out a few words here and a few words there, and pieced them together into brand-new tapes."

"Exactly. So when the spliced tapes are played back, they sound like calls for help."

Bud scowled angrily. "Of all the dirty tricks! Boy, would I like to get my hands on those rats!"

"I want to as much as you, so I can find Dad and Ted. Well, maybe we can," Tom murmured thoughtfully.

"How?" Bud asked.

"Are you game to do a little more exploring?"

"Sure. But what do we look for?" Bud queried.

"Signs of an enemy camp," Tom replied. "If they're waiting for the *Challenger* to make a landing, they may have a base somewhere within striking distance. If we could find it, we might be able to get the jump on them—at least they wouldn't be able to take us by surprise."

Bud agreed eagerly. "Now you're talking, pal!"

Hastily the boys returned to the ship to refill their oxygen tanks from the ship's supply before starting out on reconnaissance. The men were astounded when they learned about Tom's findings. They were about evenly divided in their opinion of the boys continuing their search.

"I know how you feel," said Arv. "And you're doing this partly for protection to all of us. But for goodness' sake be careful."

Chow was very much excited at thought of the dangerous mission. "Brand my asteroids, boss, you're askin' for trouble," the cook protested.

"Don't do it, Tom—it's too risky! Those ornery human steers may be fixin' to stampede you!"

"Don't worry, Chow." Tom put his hand on the cook's shoulder. "We'll try not to take any unnecessary chances. But we *must* find Dad and Ted!"

Chow shook his head uneasily. "I still think you're makin' a mistake, Tom."

Disregarding the Texan's protests, the boys climbed back into their space suits and shoved off again on their repelatron donkeys.

"Let's try that range of hills," Tom suggested, pointing to the left. "They look as if they might offer some good hiding places. Our enemy may be lurking in them."

"Okay."

Flying about fifty feet above the ground, the boys skimmed over the lunar landscape. Rocks, crags, and canyons were etched in sharp detail under the pitiless glare of sunlight. The terrain was mostly gray, tan, and rust-colored.

"There's another crater on our right," Bud signaled. "Want to swing over for a look?"

At that moment their flying platforms were approaching a deep crevasse.

"Sure, might as well," Tom responded. "Keep your eyes open for a—"

His words changed to a startled cry, taken up by Bud, as their repelatron platforms suddenly tipped. The next moment, the boys toppled from their flying donkeys and plummeted straight toward the abyss!

CHAPTER XVI

TRAPPED IN THE ABYSS

"USE your jet pistol, Bud!" Tom cried urgently over his radio.

Both boys triggered their suit jets repeatedly as they plunged downward. The blasts served to brake their fall somewhat, but were not powerful enough to hold them in mid-air.

"No use," thought Bud despairingly.

Turning and twisting, the boys plunged into the crevasse, struck the sloping sides, and caromed downward. With stunning impact, they landed at the bottom of the chasm!

For several moments Tom and Bud lay still. Fortunately, the moon's low gravity had greatly lessened the force of their fall. Their pressurized space suits and tough plastic helmets had also protected them from cuts and bruises.

Presently Tom revived enough to struggle to his feet. "Whew!" he gasped dizzily.

It was pitch dark in the narrow chasm, except for the faint glimmer of starlight above. Tom switched on his suit flashlight. The yellow glow revealed Bud's prostrate figure a few yards away.

"Bud!" Tom called, groping his way toward his companion. "Bud, are you all right?"

There was no answer, but the copilot stirred painfully. Tom helped him to stand upright. Through Bud's transparent helmet, Tom could see his lips moving, but no sound broke the eerie silence. Dismayed, Tom realized their radios must have been broken in the fall!

Bud also switched on his suit light. The two boys stared at each other helplessly.

"If we could only read lips!" Tom thought.

He gazed up at the sheer walls of the crevasse rising steeply on either side of them. Bud's eyes followed his glance. Then Tom pointed upward and made climbing motions. Bud nodded in response. Each of them grabbed a handhold on the jagged rocky surface and began clambering upward.

"We'd have to be human flies to make it in these getups!" Bud muttered to himself desperately.

With painful slowness the boys advanced, inch by inch. But it soon became obvious that in their cumbersome space suits their efforts to ascend were hopeless. Again and again their boots or gauntlets would scrabble for a hold on some rocky outthrust, only to slip off or have it give way under pressure. By the time they had struggled upward a few yards, both were weary and aching in every muscle.

Finally Tom beamed his suit light in Bud's direction. His friend shook his head hopelessly. With tired groans they gave up the attempt and slid back to the bottom of the crevasse.

The same thought ran through the boys' minds as they slumped, panting, to catch their breath. "If only we could take off these space suits!" Yet to do so would mean instant death in the moon's vacuum.

Meanwhile, back in the *Challenger,* Chow had been fussing and worrying ever since Tom and Bud had left. "I think we oughta go after them young'uns!" he told Bert Everett.

"Relax, Chow. They'll be all right," Bert replied.

"I sure wouldn't bet on that," Chow said. "Suppose they run into them kidnapers? Arv says he can't see the boys through the cabin window! Can't pick 'em up on the radio neither."

"So what? The skipper and Bud can take care of themselves."

"I'd feel a heap better if we could keep an eye on 'em, or at least hear 'em," Chow insisted.

Finally Bert agreed to go with Chow. After launching their repelatron donkeys from the ship's landing platform, Chow and Bert sailed off in the general direction of the mountains which Tom had intended to explore.

Suddenly the cook gave a startled gasp. "Hey, pardner! Take a look up ahead near that crack in the ground! Ain't them shiny things a couple o' flyin' donkeys?"

Bert scanned the objects below. "You're right, Chow! But what happened to the boys?"

Tom and Bud, trapped in the moon crevasse,

"I aim to find out!" Chow declared.

"Be careful," Bert warned. "I think maybe the boys got sucked down in that hole in the ground. We'll stay on this side of it."

Swooping down near the abandoned platforms, the two spacemen hurried to the edge of the crevasse and peered into the inky chasm. Due to the moon's lack of atmosphere, no sound was carried to the pair trapped below.

"Tom! Bud!" Chow called over his suit radio. "Anyone down below?"

There was no response.

Bert clutched the cook's arm and pointed. "Hey! Isn't that a light?" A feeble glow was

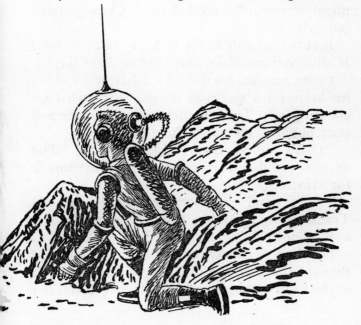

waited in helpless impatience to be rescued

barely discernible in the sun's reflected dazzle from the rocky outcroppings higher up.

Even as he spoke, the light disappeared. Tom had decided at that very moment to switch off his suit beam to conserve battery power.

"Dunno whether I saw anything or not," Chow replied, "but I reckon we'd better not pass up any chances. Tom and Bud *must* be down there, Bert, or else the two flyin' donkeys wouldn't be lyin' around."

Bert nodded. "Question is how do we get the boys out? I'd sure hate to try climbing down that straight-sided abyss."

"If Tom and Bud did fall in there, they might've cracked their helmets," Chow pointed out grimly.

Bert turned pale at the thought. "Good night! If their oxygen leaks out, they're done for!"

Chow, terrified for the boys' safety, was racking his brain for a means of rescue. "Bert, what we got to do is get Tom's matter-makin' machine and start pumpin' air down there pronto!"

"That's useless, Chow," Bert objected. "The oxygen would just drift out through the top of the crevice!"

"Don't stand there arguin', man!" the old Texan retorted. "Mebbe Arv can figure out some way to do it!"

Boarding their flying platforms, Chow and Bert sped back to the ship. Arv Hanson listened to their story and immediately decided that Tom and Bud could not climb out in their bulky space suits.

"We'll have to fix it so they can take them off," he said.

"But how?" Bert asked.

Arv suggested sealing off the whole crevice with a huge plastic dome. A number of these domes, similar to the ones Tom used for his undersea helium city, had been brought along for purposes of establishing a camp on the moon.

"Bert, move all the flying donkeys out to the landing platform!" Arv ordered. "We'll have to disassemble the solartron and transport it piece by piece. We'll need at least three of the energy collectors, too!"

Pushing the intercom button on the bulkhead, Arv barked out orders over the loud-speaker system. Two of the crewmen were detailed to stay aboard and handle the *Challenger*. Doc Simpson, who had been treating a crewman for a sudden illness, had to remain behind to administer some necessary injections. Everyone else was ordered to join the rescue party on the double.

Working with frantic speed, Arv soon had the solartron set up on the brink of the chasm. Two separate domes were erected in order to cover the whole length of the crevasse, one enclosing the machine.

While this was going on, Chow let out a yelp of joy. "Brand my prairie sunshine, there's a light down yonder! I kin see it for sure now!"

Several of the crew rushed to look. Arv signaled by waving his arms, and was delighted to see the glow of light blink off and on as Tom beamed out an "all right" in code.

"They're safe!" Chow cried out, as the crew cheered.

Meanwhile, Bert and two other men were having trouble spreading out the huge energy-collector sheets. Tom and Bud, in their underground moon prison, could only wait in helpless impatience while the difficulty was ironed out. Finally, the setup was complete and the solartron throbbed into action.

Light from the brilliant glare of one of Mr. Swift's giant searchlights flooded the chasm as current flowed from the power gatherers. Moments later, the matter maker began pouring out oxygen and nitrogen.

Tom checked the atmosphere meter on his suit and gestured to Bud when the pressure reached normal. With a joyful whoop of relief, the boys took off their helmets and doffed their space suits.

"Boy, watch me shin up that wall now!" Bud exclaimed.

Tom grinned. "Nothing to it for a couple of space monkeys like us!"

Without waiting for further assistance, the two boys began clambering up the side of the crevasse. By the time rope slings had been lowered, they were halfway to the top. Within a few moments, both Tom and Bud were sprawled safely on the dusty surface of the ground, panting as they exchanged thanks and congratulations with their rescuers.

"And now explain one thing, genius boy," Bud begged. "What happened to our repelatrons just before we crashed?"

"I have a hunch this area around the crevasse is loaded with the hydrogen compound," Tom explained, "that we detected on our last moon trip. Our donkeys weren't set to repel it."

Bud grinned. "Talk about kicking mules! Those *donkeys* really gave us the business!"

Two extra space suits had been brought along from the ship. The boys put these on and followed the crew out of the airdome.

"Before we go back," Tom suggested, "I'd like to search a little farther." He explained his theory about an enemy camp in the vicinity.

"Wal, this time you ain't goin' alone, son," Chow declared firmly. "We're *all* goin'!"

Boarding their flying platforms, the group took off, making a big detour around the chasm, and headed toward the mountains. For over an hour they searched among the crags and canyons without success. Finally, Tom thought it wise to return to the *Challenger*.

The lunar plain stretched bleak and empty in the harsh sunlight as they headed back to the spot where the ship had been hovering. At first Tom thought they were flying in the wrong direction. Then, after scanning the horizon on all sides, he realized the truth.

"Our ship is gone!" Tom cried out.

CHAPTER XVII

SURPRISE MISSILE

THERE was stunned silence as the group stared around helplessly. Had the *Challenger,* too, been captured by their enemy?

"Tom, those kidnapers may have brought your father here and forced him to fly the ship away under threat of death!" Bud suggested.

"It's possible," Tom admitted grimly. He reflected that this would fit in with his conjecture about an enemy camp close by.

"You mean we're marooned?" gulped Bert Everett.

"Don't worry. Our situation isn't hopeless." Tom pointed to the shimmering plastic domes, which were visible from the altitude of their flying platforms. "With our airdomes and the solartron, we can hold out as long as we have to."

"An' me with no cookstove!" Chow groaned. "Boss, that gelatin stuff you made tasted purty good for dessert, but I sure don't think I'm goin' to like it for a steady diet!"

Bud chuckled at the overweight cook's worried expression. "A diet's just what you need, Chow! Cheer up, old-timer! Maybe someone'll rescue us before you're down to a shadow!"

"That'll be the day," Arv said dryly, staring at the bulging contours of Chow's space suit.

To keep the men occupied, Tom suggested that they move the matter-making machine away from the crevasse. Flying to the spot, they swooped down for a landing and entered the dome which housed the machine.

"We'll have to tear down the solartron in order to move it," Tom pointed out. "So ditch your space suits, fellows."

After they had taken off the suits and helmets, Tom ordered everyone to refill his oxygen tank. Then the men grabbed wrenches and other tools and set to work disassembling the heavy machine. When the job was finished, they donned their space suits again and moved the solartron, piece by piece, to another location several hundred yards away.

"May as well leave the extra dome here," Tom decided. "We'll need only one."

The young inventor supervised the job of re-assembling the machine and shifting the dome. Then, with the energy collectors hooked up, Tom switched on power and the machine began pumping nineteen per cent oxygen, eighty per cent nitrogen, and one per cent other ingredients. Soon the airdome was filled with a livable atmosphere.

"Okay," Tom said, after glancing at his atmosphere meter to check the pressure. "Shuck your suits again and take it easy, fellows."

Two men, however, went outside to recheck the dome. The others lounged in sitting positions, or sprawled comfortably. Bert Everett suggested to Tom that they try contacting the *Challenger* by high-powered radio. The sets that they had been using in their space suits were of very low power.

Tom frowned thoughtfully. "Let's wait a while, Bert. If Doc and the others are safe, we should hear from them soon. On the other hand, if our enemy has captured the *Challenger,* a call now might give them a chance to trick us or pick up some useful information."

Arv nodded. "I agree, skipper. If the kidnapers are aboard, they'd give us a phony reply."

"I don't know about the rest of you," Bud put in, "but I could sure use a drink of water. How about putting your matter maker to work on that, Tom?"

"Sure thing, pal."

Tom adjusted the element and isotope controls. Soon the machine was pumping out a steady stream of water. The men lined up for a drink.

"Boy, does that taste good!" said Bud, wiping his mouth. "Now, what's next on the agenda?"

"Another survey outside," replied Tom, climbing into his suit. "There might be some clue around that we've missed."

The boys had just stepped from the dome when Bud yelled:

"Tom! Look!" He pointed at the sky.

A silvery missile was streaking toward them. It appeared to be headed straight toward the dome!

The crewmen, alerted, froze in fear, realizing there was no time to run from the missile. The next moment, it slowed and landed gently nearby.

"Sufferin' horned toads!" Chow quavered. "What if the thing explodes?"

Another crewman shuddered and made a dash for his space suit. "Let's get out of here!" he urged.

The others donned their suits and hurried from the dome. After rushing to a safe distance, they paused and waited for an explosion.

Minutes went by. When nothing had happened after half an hour, Tom felt it was safe to inspect the missile. "There may be a message in it for us," he told his companions.

"Think it's safe?" Arv asked dubiously.

Tom nodded. "I believe it must be harmless or it would have exploded by now. But you fellows stay back until I make sure."

The others watched anxiously as Tom walked toward the glittering object. It was a rocket of the same type as the one containing the tape recorders.

Tom opened the rocket's loading hatch and looked in. He turned pale and his companions heard him give a gasp of horror over the radio.

"It's Ted Spring!" he called. "But—"

Bud, Arv, Chow, and the other crewmen rushed forward. Their faces blanched as they saw Ted lying motionless inside the rocket. He was wearing his space suit and helmet.

"Is he—is he dead?" Bud whispered, horrified.

"I don't know. Help me lift him out," Tom replied, sick at heart.

As gently as possible, Ted was removed from the rocket and carried to the airdome, where they hastily took off his space suit and helmet. Tom, who had also removed his own heavy space gear, listened for Ted's heartbeat.

"Thank goodness! He is alive!" Tom announced.

The young inventor immediately adjusted his solartron to produce a flow of water. He began bathing Ted's face, while the others chafed the cadet's hands and wrists. But the victim showed no sign of regaining consciousness.

"Brand my oxygen mask, what's wrong with him?" Chow muttered.

Tom shrugged helplessly, gripped by a feeling of despair. "I can't even guess, Chow. And the worst of it is, we have no way to help him—not even a first-aid kit! If only Doc were here!"

"But why did the kidnapers send him back to us in this condition?" Bert puzzled. "To scare us off the chase?"

Equally puzzled, Tom replied, "I don't know the answer to that one either, Bert."

Bud scowled and clenched his fists. "If Ted dies, those rats will pay for it!"

"Wait a minute," put in Arv Hanson. "Maybe they sent a message along with him. Let's search his clothes!"

They went through Ted's pockets but found nothing. Bud and Bert now hurried outside to check the rocket for any clue. They came back and reported failure.

Time dragged by with no change in Ted's condition. The group's feelings of gloom and despair deepened. With no atmosphere or clouds on the moon to shield them, the stark glare of sunlight soon made the air inside the dome stifling hot.

"We'll have to move again," Tom decided. "We can find a place with some shade over in those mountains."

Arv and Bud made a brief reconnaissance on flying donkeys, skirting the abyss. They returned with news that they had found a shallow cave big enough to contain the dome.

"Okay," Tom said. "Let's get busy, fellows."

Hot, dejected, and streaming with perspiration, the crewmen once again disassembled the solartron and power gatherers. Fortunately, when they dressed to emerge from the dome, the air-conditioning equipment in their space suits afforded them some relief.

Ted was taken to the cave first. Bud flew the engineer's inert form on a flying donkey. The others loaded the equipment onto the platforms, and transported it to the new site. The energy collectors and the dome itself were more difficult to move, but these too were finally shifted and installed in place.

With the solartron in operation, the dome soon filled with a livable air supply. By skillfully adjusting the condensing system on the matter maker, Tom was able to heat the air to a comfortable temperature. Wearily the crewmen doffed their space suits and relaxed. Then Tom made several types of simple food which Chow proceeded to concoct into fairly tasty dishes.

"Not bad, old-timer," Bud approved as everyone ate the meal with a hearty appetite. "The way my stomach was feeling that tasted almost as good as a steak!"

Chow smiled, pleased at the compliment, but added, "Don't thank me. Thank Tom. If 'twarn't for his contraption there, we wouldn't have no grub at all!"

The men soon fell asleep, exhausted by their grueling activities. At last only Tom remained awake. The young inventor was torn with anxiety, not only for Ted and his father, but for the safety of his whole crew.

"Perhaps I should try calling the *Challenger* now," Tom decided. Switching on his suit radio, he spoke into the microphone:

"Tom calling the *Challenger!* . . . Tom calling *Challenger!* . . . Come in, please!"

Repeated efforts brought no response. After half an hour, Tom gave up and turned off the set. Glumly he stared out of the cave opening.

A few moments later he gasped. A huge boxlike spaceship, enclosed in gleaming rails, was sailing into view across the sky!

"The *Challenger!*" Tom yelled. Pulling on his space suit in frantic haste, he emerged from the dome and rushed out of the cave.

Tom waved his arms wildly, hoping to attract attention. At the same time, he signaled repeatedly over his mike. Bud and the others, awakened by his yell, joined him just in time to see the spaceship pass out of sight beyond the towering mountain peaks.

"She's g-g-gone!" Chow wailed dismally.

The same frightening thoughts ran through every mind. Had they lost their only chance of rescue? Also, was the *Challenger* perhaps now under the command of their mysterious enemy, who intended to abandon them to their fate?

CHAPTER XVIII

A STRANGE CAPTURE

TOM clenched his jaw grimly, trying not to show despair as he met the dismayed looks of his comrades. "Let's not jump to conclusions," he said. "Maybe—"

He broke off as a new thought struck him. "Wait a minute!" Tom cried. "I was radioing the ship before it appeared. Could be my battery's run down and the signal didn't carry. Try your set, Bud!"

The copilot hastily complied. "Bud Barclay calling the *Challenger*! Can you read me? . . . . Barclay to *Challenger*! Come in, please."

"*Challenger* to Barclay! *Where are you?*" It was the voice of the ship's regular radioman!

The little group of stranded explorers leaped and hugged each other in a frenzy of joy as Bud replied, "You just passed us, Marty! We're on the other side of the mountain! Come back and you'll spot us easily enough!"

The radioman explained that all was well

aboard ship. It had not been forced away or boarded. While the others were rescuing Tom and Bud, those on the ship had heard a strange jargon of voices over the radio and a blip had been picked up on the radarscope. Doc, alarmed, had ordered a crewman to race the *Challenger* out of range of attack.

"It's probably lucky you did," said Bud. "We'll bring our donkeys toward the ship."

The *Challenger* came to meet them and soon Tom and his party were trooping safely aboard. They carried with them the still-unconscious figure of Ted Spring.

"Great Scott! Where did you find him?" Doc Simpson exclaimed as they removed Ted's helmet and space suit. Pale and scarcely appearing to breathe, Ted was laid gently in a bunk.

Tom told about the landing of the second missile and how they had found Ted inside it. "You must save him, Doc," Tom begged.

"I'll do my best," the medic promised gravely.

While the young physician worked over his unconscious patient, Tom went outside again to supervise the transfer of the solartron and the power gatherers aboard the *Challenger*. When he returned to the ship's bunkroom, Ted was stirring faintly and seemed to have a better color.

"I believe he's suffering from an overdose of truth serum," Doc Simpson explained.

"Why so?" Tom asked with a puzzled frown.

"You remember that I gave Ted and your father, as well as you and Bud, injections of *anti-*

truth serum?" When Tom nodded, Doc said, "Well, I suspect that the kidnapers tried to make Ted talk, but found him immune to their truth drug. When he refused to reveal any secrets, they probably kept increasing the dosage until he lapsed into unconsciousness."

Tom was horror-struck. In a low, tight voice he asked, "Do you think you can revive him?"

"Yes, he's definitely responding," Doc Simpson replied. "Fortunately, he didn't have a fatal dose, but it may take a while for his system to throw off the effects of the drug."

Tom was still baffled as to why the kidnapers had rocketed Ted back to his friends. Was it merely to rid themselves of a useless prisoner? Or was it a part of an evil plot? In view of his enemies' ruthless methods, Tom felt the latter theory was more likely.

Suddenly Arv Hanson's voice blared out over the loud-speaker, "Tom, we're having trouble hooking up one of these energy collectors!"

Tom hurried to the hangar deck, donned his space suit, and went out through the air lock. "What's wrong?" he called over his suit radio.

Arv explained that while the collector was being shifted back to the *Challenger* from the cave setup, some of the wiring of the cell leaves had become loosened. Tom examined the wires and managed to reconnect them, although he found the job extremely difficult to do with his heavy space gauntlets.

"Hey!" exclaimed Bud, who had been watching

the operation. "Is this hail, or am I getting space-happy?"

Without warning a shower of pellets had begun raining down from the sky!

Intrigued, Tom caught a few of the pellets and examined them. They were crystalline and varied in color from steel gray to purplish black. "Looks like iodine," he muttered.

The next moment Tom gave a gasp of dismay. "Good grief!" he cried. "I just realized that these will ruin the aluminum foil of the collector tubing!"

"You said it, skipper!" Arv exclaimed. "Take a look!"

Holes had already appeared in the foil at several points, and the tubes were snaking into motion as the helium gas escaped!

"What'll we do?" asked Bud tersely, turning to Tom for orders.

Tom glanced around. The strange shower was affecting only two of the power gatherers.

"We'll repair them at once," he replied. "Men, go back to the ship quick and get some Tomasite plastic to patch the holes! Make it snappy, all of you! The iodine may attack our space suits, too!"

The crewmen needed no second warning. They dashed back to the ship and waited on the hangar deck while the patches were being prepared. Tom and Bud joined them.

"Good thing your dad invented this plastic," Bud remarked.

Tom nodded. "Best insulation there is against radiation or electromagnetic effects. And it's impervious to most known chemicals."

As soon as the patches were ready, each man was given a supply of bonding cement. Then they rushed outside and began hastily repairing the damage.

"Hurry!" Tom urged the crew over his radio. "And keep an eye on your space suits. If you spot a leak in your suit, slap a patch on it and get back to the ship pronto!"

The job was completed in a few minutes. But even before the last hole in the tubing was patched, the iodine shower had ceased.

"Wow!" Bud gasped. "I'm sure glad that's over. Where do you suppose the stuff came from, skipper? Another stunt of our enemies?"

Tom shook his head, thoroughly puzzled. "You've got me, pal."

Back aboard the *Challenger,* Tom opened the stopcocks on the helium tanks and pumped more gas into the tubing to make up for the leakage. Then, elevatoring to his laboratory, he checked some of the crystals with a Swift spectroscope. As he had surmised, they were iodine.

"I'll analyze them even more minutely when I have a chance," he told himself.

Just then, a call over the intercom summoned the young inventor to the ship's bunkroom. "Ted has just recovered consciousness," Doc Simpson reported. "He's ready to tell us what happened."

"Be down in a jiffy!" Tom replied excitedly.

A shower of pellets rained down from the sky

The patient was sitting up in his bunk, finishing a bowl of hot soup, as Tom entered. "Hi, skipper!" he said cheerfully.

Tom shook hands with him warmly. "You don't know how glad I am to see you well and safe, Ted!" he exclaimed. "Sure you feel like talking?"

"You bet!" Ted declared firmly. "The sooner I tell you everything, the sooner we can rescue your dad!"

Tom's pulse raced with hope. "Let's have it, Ted!"

"Well, your father and I were working outside the space station," Ted began, "when it happened. We had just finished adjusting the electrodes and were talking about the cosmic dust experiment, when all of a sudden we noticed we were being drawn away from the outpost. Apparently it was being done by some kind of force ray, and our jet pistols couldn't counteract it. We tried to call for help, but couldn't get any response over our radios."

"That's easily explained," said Tom. "The force ray probably caused interference."

Ted went on to relate that he and Mr. Swift had eventually been seized and taken aboard a spaceship far from the outpost. "There were only three men piloting the ship," Ted added, "but they kept us covered with ray guns until they had us aboard with our hands tied."

"Americans?" Tom asked.

Ted shook his head. "I'm not sure of their nationality, but they looked Mongolian and spoke

English with a thick accent. Anyhow, they went into orbit somewhere thousands of miles above the space station."

"But we looked everywhere," Tom said.

Ted smiled. "Those fellows are mighty clever, Tom. They knew that and kept one jump ahead of you."

"Go on with your story," Tom urged.

"Later on, two other men came aboard from another ship and tried to make your father and me talk," said Ted. "They were after the secrets of your solartron."

Ted explained that his captors had mistaken him for Tom, and were furious when they learned their error. As Doc Simpson had suspected, when the Americans refused to talk, the criminals had kept on injecting doses of truth serum.

"After a while I blacked out," Ted concluded. "That's the last I remember."

"What about Dad?"

Ted shrugged unhappily. "I'm sorry, Tom, but I just don't know. All I can tell you is that he seemed okay just before I got woozy and passed out. Keep your chin up though, skipper! I'm sure we can find their rocket, because I know where it's orbiting!"

"How come?" Tom asked eagerly. "Did they reveal their position?"

"Not exactly," Ted replied. "But from what they said, I do know they're planning to stay in the same orbit. It seems they cooked up this whole plot against you without the knowledge of their government, so they don't dare land any-where with either of us aboard. Their object is to learn the plans for your matter maker, and then palm it off as their own invention."

"But how does that help us find their posi-tion?" Tom asked worriedly.

"I'm coming to that," said Ted. "They took our watches away a while after we came aboard, but not before we learned that they always served our meals at regular intervals. That enabled us to judge the passing of time pretty well."

Tom nodded. "And?"

"Your dad and I could tell, from glimpses we caught of the earth every so often, how long it was taking us to orbit. We found out that we passed over the same spot on earth every two and a half days."

Tom slammed his fist into his palm. "Smart work, Ted! That clue identifies the height of their orbit! We'll take off as soon as the ship is ready!"

CHAPTER XIX

FLAG OF TRUCE

AS TOM rushed to the wall panel and pushed the alarm button signaling a general alert, he had never been more excited in his life.

"Attention, everyone!" he shouted over the intercom. "Ted has just told me that my father is being held prisoner on an enemy rocket. We'll try to intercept it. As soon as the *Challenger* can be made ready, we'll take off! You getting this, Arv?"

"Sure am, skipper," came the reply.

"All right. Check the solartron, the energy collectors, and see that the ship's repelatrons are okay. Everything must be in top working condition. Then muster all hands and make sure everybody's aboard. Report when you're ready."

"Roger!" Arv acknowledged.

Tom made some quick calculations as he hurried back to Ted Spring's bunk. He knew that the observed time of two and a half days to circle the earth would fix the enemy ship's distance above our planet, since a body's orbital rate varied at different altitudes.

"Ted, what was the spot on earth you used as a reference point and when did you first see it?" Tom asked.

"It was the western bulge of Africa," Ted replied. "The first time we passed over the area it was approximately seven A.M. on the morning after we were captured. We appeared to be moving east southeast."

"Good! I'll work the rest out by computer!"

Tom hurried to the ship's computer room and fed in the data which Ted had just given him. He added the orbital period of sixty hours and the elapsed time since the first observation. In a twinkling the navigation dials on the electronic brain showed the enemy rocket's present celestial latitude and longitude, as well as its distance from the earth, which was about 60,000 miles.

Tom grinned with satisfaction, then flicked a switch and pressed a "memory" button. The computer would now retain this information and continue calculating the rocket's movement after the *Challenger* took off.

"I'd better see how Arv's making out," Tom said to himself as he hurried out of the compartment.

Going down in the elevator, he was struck by a new thought. He donned his space suit hastily in the hangar compartment and went out through the air lock, meeting Bud on the landing platform outside.

"Where to, skipper?" Bud asked over his suit radio.

"Bud, when you and Bert looked for a message in that rocket which carried Ted, did you search it thoroughly?" Tom asked.

"Well, sure . . . at least, I *think* so," Bud replied. "Why?"

"Because I have a hunch there must have been a message somewhere aboard," Tom asserted. "Otherwise, why would the kidnapers bother to send Ted back? I doubt if those guys were just being kind!"

"Not that bunch!" Bud agreed. "Okay. Let's look again."

The two boys boarded flying carpets and soared off toward the spot where the missile was still lying.

When they landed beside the rocket, Tom said, "Bud, you check the outer surface. Make sure there's nothing scratched or stamped on the metal. I'll look inside."

Several minutes went by while the boys examined every inch of the missile. Tom was about ready to give up, then decided to take another look in a crevice in front of the loading hatch. This time he gave a whoop of triumph.

"I've found it, Bud!" The young inventor held up a small plastic case containing a rolled-up paper. In the boys' haste to remove Ted, they must have knocked it from the holder above the door. Tom opened it and read a message printed in English:

TOM SWIFT JR. IF YOU WISH TO HAVE
YOUR FATHER RETURNED SAFELY, OBEY
THESE ORDERS. LEAVE THE COMPLETE
PLANS, DRAWINGS, AND CALCULATIONS
FOR YOUR MATTER-MAKING MACHINE IN-
SIDE THIS ROCKET. YOU AND YOUR ENTIRE
CREW MUST THEN LEAVE THE MOON AND
RETURN TO YOUR SPACE OUTPOST. YOUR
FATHER WILL BE SENT THERE BY ROCKET
AS SOON AS THE PLANS ARE IN OUR HANDS.
IF YOU DO NOT COMPLY, YOU WILL NEVER
SEE YOUR FATHER ALIVE AGAIN!

The message carried no signature. Tom's eyes
misted and his throat constricted for a moment.
But Bud gave a snort of fury. "Those sneaking
space rats!" he gritted. "Tom, you're not going
to give in to them, are you?"

"Of course not. Dad wouldn't want me to,"
Tom retorted grimly. "Come on. Let's get back to
the ship! I want to take off before I blow my top!"

While flying back to the *Challenger,* Tom
checked with Arv Hanson by radio and learned
that the ship was ready and the crew mustered.
On reaching the space craft Tom told him briefly
about the ransom note, then hurried up to the
flight compartment with Bud. A few moments
later the mighty space cruiser took off from the
moon area.

"Automatic pilot all the way?" Bud asked as the
Challenger zoomed through the void.

Tom nodded. "The computer will guide us to
the interception point. We should meet their

orbital track somewhere above the Indian Ocean."

Hours went by. As the time for interception approached, Tom passed the word over the intercom. Mike watched the radarscope intently.

"No sign of 'em, skipper," he reported after scanning the area carefully for ten minutes.

Tension mounted with every passing moment. Tom clenched his jaw in disappointment as the enemy rocket ship failed to appear.

"I can't understand it, Tom!" Ted Spring groaned. He blamed himself for the failure. Hopefully he added, "Maybe they've gone back to earth."

Tom preferred not to think of this angle. It might mean his father was dead or beyond hope of rescue. "Look, Ted," he said, "are you *positive* you sighted the same spot on earth each time?"

Ted shrugged hopelessly. "As sure as I can be. Of course the area was partly blotted out by cloud drifts, and I caught only a few quick glimpses. But it certainly looked like the African coast. Why, I could even make out the line of mountains!"

"Mountains?" Tom repeated. "Can you draw me a map?"

"Sure." Ted sketched out the contours of the land mass which he had seen, and shaded in the topography roughly.

"Those mountains were the Andes, Ted!" the young inventor exclaimed. "You must have been looking at South America!"

"South America?" Ted was thunderstruck.

Tom nodded. "Both South America and Africa have much the same coast outline. The two continents each bulge at the top and taper down to a narrow point at the southern tip. It would be easy to confuse them. Let's refigure our calculations for the orbital track, assuming my hunch is correct!"

Turning over the controls to Bud, the young inventor hurried to the computer room with Ted. Here he fed in a new set of data. Then, as the electronic brain altered its flow of impulses to the navigational instruments, Tom returned to the flight comparment and slid back into the pilot's seat.

Bud flashed him a questioning look. "Got the new course figured, Tom?"

"Right! Keep your fingers crossed, pal!"

At lightning speed they arced through the vast reaches of space, thousands of miles above the terrestrial atmosphere. Below, they watched the turning ball of earth, with its tapestry of oceans and continents.

Suddenly the intercom buzzed. "I've picked up something, skipper!" the radarman reported. "Looks like a rocket ship, dead ahead!"

The news electrified the crew. Within minutes Arv had sighted the craft by telescope, and soon it became visible through the pilots' windows.

"That's it!" Ted cried out. "I'm sure that's our enemy's rocket!"

Tom flicked on the radio and spoke into his microphone. "Swift ship *Challenger* calling

nearby rocket! This is Tom Swift Jr. speaking!
. . . Swift to nearby rocket! . . . Come in,
please!"

His call was followed by silence. Tom tried
several frequencies but still got no response.

"They're playing possum," Bud muttered.

Tom nodded grimly, maintaining his course
straight toward the enemy. Suddenly a rocket
port opened in the ship's side. There was a burst
of smoke and flame as a missile came streaking
toward the *Challenger!*

"They're firing at us!" Bud yelled.

Tom's hand shot toward the control panel,
tuning up the antimeteor repelatron to full
power. Instantly the missile was held immobile
by the ship's force wave! Losing momentum, it
plunged out of orbit, eventually to burn up in
the earth's atmosphere.

"Terrific, skipper!" Ted cheered, as the crew
joined in.

Again the enemy rocket spurted flame, and
other missiles followed. All rebounded harm-
lessly from the *Challenger's* invisible shield. To
ensure ample protection against the barrage, Tom
brought two of his main repelatron radiators
into play. At last the firing ceased.

"Looks as though they're giving up!" Bud
chuckled.

Tom's face became grave. "Bud, I'm worried.
If they figure they can't hold out against us, they
may decide to kill Dad rather than be taken
alive!"

"Good night! I never thought of that!" The copilot stared at Tom fearfully. "What can we do?"

"I'll try calling them again!" But as Tom began speaking into his mike, a white flag suddenly appeared from the air lock of the enemy rocket!

"A flag of truce!" Bud cried. "They must be ready to surrender!"

The young inventor scowled thoughtfully.

"A flag of truce!" Bud cried.

"That white flag may be a trick, but there's only one way to find out," he replied. "I'll go aboard."

"And I'll go with you!" Bud volunteered.

"Okay. Arv, you take over. Keep a sharp watch and be ready for trouble."

"Roger!"

Donning space suits, the two boys left the *Challenger* and propelled themselves toward the enemy craft. The rocket's air lock opened to admit them.

"Guess the welcome mat is out," Bud remarked, with a quizzical glance at his companion.

"They must be ready to surrender!"

Tom shrugged, tight-lipped, and went in through the hatch. Bud followed. As the outer door closed behind them, the inner door of the air lock opened. The boys paused cautiously and removed their space helmets before stepping into the ship's living compartment. Before they could draw back, strong hands seized the two boys and yanked them inside!

"So sorry," hissed a voice with a thick Mongolian accent, "but Mr. Swift is not here. You will please hand over the complete plans now. Then we will tell you what happened to him!"

CHAPTER XX

A RACE TO THE RESCUE

THE boys glared angrily at their captors. The man who had spoken was a short, squat fellow with Asiatic features. His two companions also appeared to be Mongolians. One was nearly bald except for a few strands of black hair brushed across his shiny skull. The other was tall and thin, with catlike amber eyes.

"What's the big idea?" Bud blazed, ready to take on all three with his fists. "Are you guys—"

"Hold it, Bud!" Tom put a restraining hand on his friend's arm. Turning to the leader of the enemy trio, Tom added coldly, "Have you forgotten about that flag of truce you showed?"

With a sneer the man replied, "International law does not carry into space. Besides, I am doing no harm. I am simply offering you a bargain. And I must remind you, my dear Tom Swift, that you and your friend are now our prisoners!"

Despite a feeling of uneasiness, Tom maintained a bold front. "You're wrong!" he retorted.

"You three are *our* prisoners any time we feel like taking over this ship."

"Exactly what do you mean?" The man's tone was suddenly different.

"Your missiles can't harm us, and you can't get away. Our ship can outspeed this rocket easily. What's more," Tom pointed out, "I have a large enough crew to overpower you three in a hurry. And they'll do just that if my friend and I aren't allowed to leave this rocket safely!"

Apparently his words struck home. The enemy trio glanced at one another in alarm. Some of the bluster seemed to leave the short, squat leader.

"Please! Let us talk sense," he urged Tom. "You have something we want, and we can supply information that you want. Why not co-operate?"

"If that means giving you the secret of my matter maker, it's out of the question!" Tom snapped. "Tell me, where's my father? You'd better produce him fast! And who are you?"

The stranger, who refused to give his name or that of his companions, answered noncommittally, "The truth is, we cannot produce your esteemed father because he is no longer aboard this ship."

"It is true," the other two men chimed in, nodding their heads vigorously.

The young inventor felt a pang of alarm. "Then where is he?" Tom demanded.

"He disappeared several hours ago." The enemy leader explained that Mr. Swift had complained of feeling ill. He had begged to put on his space suit and go outside for exercise after his long, cramped imprisonment aboard the rocket. "We knew he could not get far with only the reaction pistol on his space suit," the Mongolian continued, "so we granted his request."

"Well, what happened?" Tom said impatiently.

"Suddenly a strange-looking spaceship appeared. It drew your father inside, and sped off. We tried to follow it and recapture him, using our own force ray. But we were unable to overtake the other craft or draw it to us. It traveled at incredible speed!"

Tom asked what the strange ship looked like. The man replied that it was flat and saucer-shaped, and made of polished blue-green metal, with no apparent openings other than the sliding panel through which Mr. Swift had been taken aboard.

Tom and Bud shot each other glances of comprehension. "Sounds like the space ark!" Bud murmured, referring to the mysterious craft in which the space people had sent their infected animals.

Tom felt an inward surge of jubilation. He was sure that the rescue ship must belong to his space friends. Apparently they had at last responded to his pleas for help or information!

"But this story may just be a hoax," Tom told himself.

To rule out any further chance of trickery, Tom insisted upon searching the enemy rocket ship. The men agreed, but as they had claimed, Mr. Swift was not aboard.

"One more question," Tom said. "Just before my father asked to go outside, did anything unusual happen?" The young inventor was somewhat puzzled as to how Mr. Swift could have known beforehand that he was about to be rescued.

"Most strange that you should ask," the squat Mongolian replied with a puzzled frown. "As a matter of fact, some queer-looking symbols flashed on the oscilloscope of our radio equipment. Shortly after your father saw them he made his request to go outside."

Tom and Bud wanted to shout for joy but remained calm. Both realized that the space people must have sent Mr. Swift a message, knowing that his captors would be unable to translate it.

"We'll go now," Tom told the three kidnapers. "From here on, you can answer to your own government. I advise you to rocket back to earth immediately. If that saucer ship returns and finds you still here, I warn you there may be unpleasant consequences!"

By this time, the three kidnapers were reduced to trembling agitation. "You must help us!" their leader pleaded. "We dare not go back to our own country and face the other members of our group! It might mean death to all of us for bungling this affair and losing our hostage!"

"What is your country, and who are the other members of your group?" Tom demanded.

The three men refused to answer this question. From their evasive replies, Tom suspected that the group might be made up of renegade scientists of several nationalities, with headquarters in the country from which these men came.

"There's one kind of help we can give you," Tom said. "The United States authorities may extend you some kind of protection." Tom did not express aloud his following thought, "In exchange perhaps for the plans of your force ray!"

The kidnapers remained silent. Tom, eager to overtake his father, went on, "I'll look you up on the return trip. Make up your mind. Come on, Bud! Let's get back to our own ship."

The crestfallen trio of kidnapers made no effort to interfere as the two young Americans donned their space helmets and went out through the air lock. Thoroughly elated, Tom and Bud started back to the *Challenger*.

"I'd hate to be in those guys' shoes!" Bud chuckled. "The important thing, though, is that your dad's safe. I'm sure glad."

"So am I," Tom replied. "Only one thing I can't figure."

"What's that, pal?"

"Why didn't we pick up that rescue message from the space people on our own ship?"

"I was wondering that myself," Bud said.

Tom was thoughtful as they reached the *Challenger's* landing platform. "Perhaps our space friends used a highly focused directional beam," he mused. "If so, that would explain it."

Once inside, the boys were besieged with excited questions from Arv, Ted, and the crew.

Tom reported his parley with the kidnapers, and his plan to rescue Mr. Swift. Everyone cheered.

"Now I must find out from the space people where to pick up Dad," Tom concluded.

The young inventor hurried to the radio room, accompanied by Bud, and beamed out a query over the ship's powerful transmitter. Moments later, the reply from his space friends began flashing on the oscilloscope.

Tom translated the mathematical symbols from memory, scribbling words at top speed. The complete message read:

SPACESHIP WITH YOUR FATHER ABOARD IS
HEADED ON COURSE TO ORBIT AROUND
VENUS. SPEED 40,500 MILES PER HOUR.

"Wow!" Bud gasped. "Forty thousand, five hundred miles per hour! Any chance of catching it?"

Tom nodded. "I'm sure we can, even though the rocket has a head start of about six hours. The *Challenger* can hit faster speeds than that and also, unlike rockets, can accelerate for long periods of time."

"Let's see," said Bud. "How far away from the earth *is* Venus?"

"It can be as close as twenty-six million miles, or as far as a hundred and nineteen million miles."

"Some trip we're about to make!" Bud commented.

"It's all right, pal." Tom chuckled, slapping his friend on the back. "With our matter maker aboard, we can chase that saucer clear across the solar system if we have to!"

After snapping out orders over the intercom, Tom hurried to the flight compartment. He set the controls of the *Challenger* for the required rate of acceleration and the ship streaked off in pursuit of the rescue craft. Their speed increased at fifty feet per second per second.

After two hours, the *Challenger* was approximately in the position that Mr. Swift's rocket had been when Tom had begun the pursuit.

"Dad's about eighty thousand miles straight ahead," he said to Bud. "Right now our speed is seventy miles per second. "We'll have to start slowing down, so we'll be going the same speed he is when we catch up to him."

"I get it," the copilot said, then added quizzically, "Better not put on the brakes all at once, chum!"

Tom grinned. "Don't worry. I'm decelerating now—by degrees."

The young inventor took time out to radio Ken Horton at the outpost and inform him of the latest developments.

"That's great news," said Horton. "Best of luck, Tom. We'll be waiting further word from you. By the way, I have some news from Enterprises."

The outpost commander went on, "Ames says to tell you that they've nailed the person who tampered with the papers for the *Journal* while they were on Miss Warner's desk."

"Who was it?"

"Some new employee named Amberson Lintner. Ames says this Amby has been taken into custody and that Miss Warner is in a state of collapse over her carelessness in the office and her friendship with him."

Ames had said that on the pretext of wanting to date the secretary, Amby would come to her desk. Then, when she was not looking, he would sneak into the Swifts' private office and pick up information. Once he had almost been caught— he was the eavesdropper who had bumped into the shelves of bottles and models of inventions.

Amby had also been responsible for the marred printing plates and had made up the story of the dog being the cause of the "accident." The disloyal employee had been working with a crooked lawyer using the alias of Hampshire and both men had become dupes of a foreign ring.

"The ones we're going to look up on the way back to earth are part of the group," Tom said.

Horton added that both Amby and Hampshire in their underhanded work had concentrated on Ted Spring in order to get secret information about the solartron from him. Both had phoned Ted and had also deliberately planned the car accident. Furthermore, a recheck on the servo units in Mr. Spring's cracked-up test plane had upheld the original findings. The accident was not the result of any carelessness on the part of the Swifts.

"Hampshire thought Ted would fall for his

story right away," said Ken Horton. "By the way, Hampshire is in jail."

As Horton continued, Tom learned that the unscrupulous scientist members of the foreign group had been traced and exposed by patiently checking every name on the *Journal's* mailing list. Receiving the design equation for the solartron had whetted the group's appetite for further knowledge of Tom's marvelous invention. They had planned the double kidnaping as a means of extorting the complete plans for the machine.

"Dad sure will be glad to hear all this," Tom declared when Horton had concluded. "Thanks for the report, Ken."

He had no sooner said "Roger" than another news flash came, this time from the Mongolians. They were going back to their own country!

"Probably it's just as well," Tom commented.

"And you'll invent a better force-ray machine," Bud consoled him.

"It's a challenge," Tom agreed.

The young inventor once more concentrated all his attention on the *Challenger's* progress.

"How close to our goal are we?" Bud asked him.

"We're down to thirty miles a second and Dad's only seventeen thousand miles ahead," Tom announced with excitement in his voice. "We're close enough to change the controls to manual."

Presently the planet Venus came into view on the space position finder screen as a small greenish dot. The next moment the radarman reported:

"Object dead ahead, skipper!"

"Your dad's rocket!" exclaimed Bud.

Minutes later, a glistening speck appeared in the inky void. It grew steadily in size, finally becoming recognizable as the disk-shaped space ark.

"Brand my moon calves, I remember now!" Chow whooped. "This is jest like that flyin' saucer what carried them sick space critters. This must be it, all right, boss!"

Tom nodded, grinning with relief. After overtaking the odd-shaped craft, he locked the *Challenger* on a parallel course alongside it. A moment later a sliding panel opened in the ark and a space-suited figure emerged into view.

"It's Dad!" Tom cried joyfully.

A minute later Mr. Swift unharmed, entered through the *Challenger's* air lock.

There was a heart-warming reunion as father and son clasped hands and embraced each other. Then Mr. Swift and Ted exchanged greetings of relief and joy.

"It's wonderful to see you all again," Mr. Swift said huskily. "Mother and Sandy all right, Tom?"

"They will be when they know you're safe and well." Tom smiled. "We'll flash the word on our way back to the outpost."

After receiving the congratulations of the crewmen and shaking hands with everyone, Mr. Swift accompanied Tom to the radio compartment. Here they sent word to the space station that the *Challenger* was heading back with Mr. Swift safely aboard.

After Tom had given his father a full account of the report from Ames relayed by Ken Horton, Mr. Swift nodded in satisfaction.

"It will be good to get home," the elder inventor said. "I've had enough adventure for a while, even without being given any more truth serum by those Mongolians. How about you, Tom?"

"After I see the folks and Phyl, I'll be ready for whatever turns up," Tom replied. His next invention and the exciting episodes that would evolve from it were not known to him at the moment, but would soon become famous as *Tom Swift and His Electronic Retroscope*.

As the *Challenger* proceeded on its way back to the outpost, Bud turned to his friend. "Well, Tom, when do we plant that colony on the moon?"

Tom laughed. "As soon as we can get ready. I have a lot of experiments and projects lined up to tackle. So, with everybody pitching in, I'm sure we *can* establish the first settlement on the moon very soon."

"*Yahoo!*" Chow cheered. "Jest *ee*-magine— livin' in the first li'l ole moon town!"

"That's the idea, Chow." Tom chuckled, and Bud added, "Dare you to make a roast beef dinner with our skipper's solartron!"